POSTMARK 9/11

The Lost Letters That Reveal The Untold Story

TARA YOUNG AND BLAKE WATSON

Postmark 9/11
The Lost Letters That Reveal The Untold Story

For information about this title or to order other books and/or electronic media, contact the publisher:
Young / Watson
P.O. Box 425 / Needham Heights, MA / 02494
www.Postmark911.com
info@Postmark911.com

ISBN: 978-0-9793216-0-3

Printed in the United States of America

Cover and Interior design: 1106 Design

Illustrations: Marina Gamble / www.marinagamble.com

Though much of the information contained in Postmark 9/11 can be researched and found to be factual, it is a work of fiction.

What The Experts Are Saying About
Postmark 9/11

"…a fascinating story that I hope will awaken the imagination of the American people to the truth about what really happened on 9/11. It has been the failure of the public to imagine the 'inconvenient truth' that is the major challenge — not a lack of explosive evidence. This story may just be the lightning rod."

— RICHARD GAGE
AIA, ARCHITECT
AE911TRUTH.ORG

"A captivating read and a welcome alternative look at the mystery surrounding the unanswered questions of September 11th. Mixing facts which — though undisputable — have long been ignored, with an intriguing narrative, this book will capture the attention of those who have never considered an alternative explanation to the events of that tragic day."

— CHRISTOPHER GRUENER MA, LMHC
IMAGINE@OURWORLDUNITED.NET

"A powerful read. Gave me pause and sent me to my computer for a night, to check on the facts. Wow! Is there no one else checking these points?"

— BERNARD WEBB
REVIEWER

Dear Reader:

On February 21, 2012, a young lady, whose identity we've chosen to keep private, arrived in our office with a box of letters she found in an old farmhouse she recently purchased. The letters captured correspondence between Tara Young and her boyfriend, Blake Watson. Since most of the letters were safely nestled in envelopes, we were able to chronologically organize their correspondence. For those letters loose in the box, we fashioned a timeline in hopes of getting the order correct.

Painstakingly, our staff and a team of forensic writing specialists verified each envelope's postmark, qualified that the stock used was available 11 years ago, and confirmed an aging process that denotes the letters were written in this time period. We can safely validate their authenticity.

We confirmed the identity of Tara Young and Blake Watson and spoke with many of their family and friends to legitimize some of the accounts noted in their letters. Indeed, Ms. Young had once worked at a NYC art gallery and Mr. Watson was once employed as a security guard for the Twin Towers. Mr. Watson's disappearance dovetails with the last known sighting of him in New York City. Ms. Young did leave her job with the art gallery at the end of January 2002, and no one has heard from her since. Mr. Rob Boswell, who you will find plays heavily in Tara and Blake's correspondence, respectfully declined our requests for an interview. He did however submit a list of websites he suggested we reference. A subset of the list Mr. Boswell provided can be found in the back of this book.

It should be noted that at the end of their correspondence, the fate of Tara and Blake is not known. We can surmise however that they were able to find each other as the letters were found bound together in a desk drawer in a rural Vermont farmhouse. We sent investigators to this locale who verified that a young couple, going by the names of Dawn and Bob, arrived at this small farmhouse with the big red barn and wide open fields, within a week of the last letter's postmark. Upon viewing photographs of the young couple, it was confirmed they were indeed Tara Young and Blake Watson. From all accounts this young couple kept to themselves and lived here for several months. Of the few residents we were able to locate who were around during this time period, there is no one who recalls what happened to them. One neighbor commented, "They just up and disappeared one day."

We wrestled with the decision to use their real names for this book. In the end, we decided any individuals Blake and Tara thought were out to harm them had enough information, including their names, that attempts on our part to conceal their identity would be superfluous. In a way, we hope shining a light on their story will encourage them to step forward.

This publishing house does not necessarily endorse what is unraveled through these letters, but rather presents the reader with an unvarnished look at Tara and Blake's communication and encourages you to draw your own conclusion. If nothing else, we ask that you entertain the idea that oftentimes what is presented is not necessarily the whole story.

"Imagination is the one weapon
in the war against reality"

— Jules de Gaultier

———•———

Tara,

You have no idea how hard it was for me to leave. I'm so sorry. But after what happened the other night at the Towers, and really what's been transpiring there for the last couple of weeks, I felt I just had to. I needed to leave the insanity of the city. You don't know how I wish you were here with me.

It's been so long since I've seen Rob, and I've never been to Maine. Maine has a beauty all its own. Really unique compared to the rest of New England that I've seen. I wish I had listened to you about getting my own cell phone though. I was so used to having the company one at my disposal I didn't realize how fast I would miss it. Especially when I needed to hear your voice. I miss just the sound of it. The comfort a few of your words can bring.

Rob said it was all right to use his house phone, but tomorrow morning we're headed to one of the cabins where Rob is a caretaker, and unfortunately there's no phone up there. The owners allow him to use the cabins anytime one is vacant, and Rob learned yesterday that the people renting it for the next two weeks had to bail. Lucky us! Rob's going to spend the weekend

Publisher's Note: The postmark on this letter's envelope is August 2, 2001

with me in the cabin, but needs to return Monday to his garage. He hadn't planned on taking any time off so I'll be all by my lonesome the next two weeks. It'll seem strange being by myself after living in NY for so long, but I'm looking forward to relaxing, if that's possible, given all that's on my mind.

You'd like Rob. He hasn't changed a wick since I last saw him strut across the stage in his half-opened graduation gown with nothing on underneath but Sponge Bob Squarepants boxer shorts. And this was at M.I.T.! He pumped his fists in the air and did a little hoochie-momma dance right before he took the diploma from the dean. What a character! He finished tops in his class and holds a PhD in a degree with a long name that I can never remember. Suffice it to say he's a brain.

In fact, he was heavily recruited by N.A.S.A., but decided instead to come up here to Maine. I asked him one time if he ever got bored fixing cars, but he just gave me a sideways grin. I mean, the guy should be designing rockets and here he is fixing the transmission on an old VW van. And that's a true statement — he is fixing one of those vans. It looks as if it never got cleaned (inside or out), and still has faded old hippie bumper stickers all over the back of it. Rob really enjoys fixing things, and coupled with his love of fishing and hunting, I can see why Maine is a good place for him.

I know how you feel about hunting and I'm not a big fan myself, but it's hard to find fault with a hunter like Rob who reminds me that I buy meat in the store and order it in a restaurant. He's just cutting out the middleman.

Wow, can't believe I'm writing a letter. It's something hardly anyone does anymore. No wonder the U.S. Postal Service is going broke. Remember when people used to watch their mailbox for that special letter? It wasn't so long ago. I'm kind of glad Rob doesn't have a computer here or I would be banging this out in no time on the keyboard. Something about the rustic nature of this place makes it seem fitting to have pen in hand.

Thank you for taking care of Rutherford while I'm gone. I hope he'll warm up to you. He is such a regal kitty.

If you need to reach me call Rob at his house phone 207-555-1234, he'll get a message to me and of course feel free to write me at Rob's address: Rob Boswell, P.O. Box 425, Saco, Maine, 02494. I know I'm only here two (maybe three?) weeks, but you never know…you might get the urge to write me!

I miss you, Tara. I miss the look on your face when I brought you flowers, the feel in my heart when you'd bring me your kiss. Did we meet at the worst possible time? Or is it the beginning of the best, Tara? I'm firmly hoping for the latter. Losing my job now doesn't help so much, but perhaps being a security guard in the Towers wasn't really my future. I can't wait to build a brand new one that includes you. It's funny how fate can change your whole life in a moment. Just five weeks ago, had I not been laid off and was able to sleep late for the first time in years, not awaken to find there was no coffee in my place, I wouldn't have walked down to the Starbucks on 57th. I would never have heard the change fall on the floor. Never turned to see you picking it up while those in line had to wait. And when I bent down to help, I would have never had the opportunity to look into those big brown eyes of yours that captivated my heart, and do to this moment. What a woman I would find in there. This short vacation is only serving to remind me how I long to look into them again.

I know we've only known each other a short time, but it feels like I've known you forever. I'll be home soon Tara.

OX

Blake

"Oftentimes instead of drawing a line,
we travel along with it so as not to
create a boundary, but to continue
the quest without restriction"

— J.R.

Blake,

I'm glad we had the opportunity to talk last night. At the risk of annoying you, would you allow me another shot at clarifying what I was trying to say? I know you heard me, but don't think my arguments were fully formed or presented well.

Look, I know it must have come as a shock to hear your apartment was broken into — no question about it. Mrs. Ward and I did the best we could putting things in some semblance of order and both agree that with the exception of Rutherford's disappearance, there really doesn't seem to be anything missing. I do agree with you, it's impossible for us to really know for sure. The cop who filled out the report thinks it was kids and I agree with him. What burglar is going to take the time to empty out your refrigerator? Who else but a kid would throw all your vanity stuff in the shower stall? Take the bedding off your bed? It just doesn't make sense that it was a burglar.

I really don't think this has anything to do with what happened at the Towers. How could those guys know who you are, much less where you live? Yes, your point about there being security cameras everywhere in the Towers has merit. They could have captured your image and matched it to your employee records, but how do you even know those guys are with the new security team? They didn't have uniforms on and never identified themselves, right?

If it was them what could they possibly gain from ransacking your place? What would they be looking for and for the sake of argument, if they are with the new security company, as you suspect, wouldn't they simply want to know what you were doing at the Towers that night? A visit to your old company isn't unusual, but rather easily explained. Still, why would they care?

I guess I just don't understand why this has shaken you so. There are a million and one break-ins every day in this city. I bet a kid in your building noticed that you'd been gone a couple of days and took the opportunity to invite his buddies over to have fun in 5C!

Please don't worry about Rutherford. I'm going to go back periodically (hope you don't mind that this will only be during daylight hours), to see if he shows up. I can't imagine that big ole' cat would allow just anyone to pick him up and squire him away. Why I was feeding him and he wouldn't even let me touch him!

Then again, how can I begrudge his behavior when I too am feeling the weight of your absence?

Here I am in a city of millions longing to find only you in the corner coffee shop, sitting beside me on the subway, or in my kitchen cooking Lamb Chippity Chops (remember you promised to share this favorite Watson recipe!).

Ah Blake, I really wish we had a different conversation last night. Were your apartment not ransacked I would have told you how I think of you every moment of the day.

xo

Tara

"A timid person is frightened before a danger, a coward during the time, and a courageous person afterward"

— Jean Paul Richter

My Tara,

How I wish that all I had to deal with was the burning ember of our romance. But my heart has to share those blissful thoughts with this unsavory smorgasbord of intruding emotions. What a comfort your presence would be right now. There is so much to say, and really I'm afraid to. I don't know where to begin.

It all has to do with that evening I went back to the Towers to clean a few things out of my locker.

I don't want to worry you too much from afar but there is a lot more about that evening I purposely haven't said. That is, until now. And so you know, Tara, I don't feel comfortable talking about this over the phone, which is the reason this information is all being brought out in my letter. Since staying here at the cabin, the only phone available to me is in a public area and I'm afraid someone will overhear my conversation. What I'm about to tell you is not for public consumption.

The night I went back to the Towers to get the rest of my stuff, I ran into my good friend, Joe. He was sorry management let me go and told me he missed seeing my ugly mug around the place. We decided we'd go down to Sullivans and get a couple cold ones. As I was cleaning out my locker, he told me about hearing these incredibly loud noises in the office above him that afternoon. He said it was like someone was moving heavy equipment across the floor. Well he knew the floor above his, like many floors in the Towers, was completely unoccupied. Is it possible I heard of a new tenant coming in? Usually we were given sixty-day notice when a new tenant was to arrive. I passed it off as possibly being workmen on the floor fixing the air conditioning or something and Joe laughed. Telling me I was dreaming. No simple fix of an air conditioning unit would create that amount of noise. One thing led to another and I must admit my interest was piqued. I suggested we go up and take a look around.

We got up there and found the floor empty. At first. At the very end of the hallway we found crates marked "Explosives," lined up against the wall. Then all of a sudden there was gunfire blasting through the hall. Yes, we were shot at! We ran like HELL. I felt Joe beside me as we bolted, but then realized he was no longer there when I reached the stairwell door. With bullets still flying, I took off. I took every diversion and shortcut I knew in my flight from that building, and when I got outside I didn't stop. I made my way over to Sullivans praying that Joe would join me there. Just hoping he found another way out, but that was not to be. I paced and panicked around the place for a bit, then I decided to call his cell phone. It rang a few times before someone picked up…but didn't say a word. I shouted into the phone, "Joe" "Joe", but there was no answer. Sullivans was busy that night so it may be that I couldn't hear him with the payphones being in back by the restrooms. But then Joe's phone was hung up or disconnected.

Tara, I can't tell you how my heart sank. When I left Sullivans, my mind was spinning in every direction, my emotions unrecognizable to myself. As a security guard I had witnessed a lot of knucklehead behavior in the Towers, but this was unfathomable. Who would shoot at us? What happened to my dear friend? When I could think straight I decided to head home and get my security guard credentials before going to see the police. I thought it would give some legitimacy to my being there in the building when I really had no actual authorization.

When I got to my building there were a couple dark cars parked haphazardly out front, but in my haste, I didn't think anything of it. I climbed up the five flights of stairs and when I got to that little alcove on the landing, I heard voices. Sneaking a peek around the corner I saw three men right outside my apartment door. They were dressed in suits and appeared to be jimmying the lock on my door, I really couldn't tell. I quietly headed back down the stairs, frantic and wondering what the HELL is going on. I don't know why, I guess that it was out of fear, but I decided to get my endangered ass out of there. I went out the back exit of the building. My first instinct was to head to the bus station. Without a car, what other choice did I have? My mind was thinking only of escape. I got to the station and quickly checked the schedule for any departures. I saw one departing in about a half hour heading north to Maine. It was the longest half hour of my life, with most of the time spent in the bathroom hiding out. I had a feeling "they" might look for me at the station.

Before I left, I knew I had to call the police to tell them what happened at the Towers. They told me as a material witness I could either meet them at the Towers or they would come pick me up. After what I had been through, the last thing I wanted to do was go back there. Besides, my bus was minutes away from leaving. Frightened that my life was in danger, I said, "You go check it out!" and hung up the phone. I boarded the bus thinking of Joe, and thought I could deal with this better from a safe distance. When the bus was finally pulling out of the station I felt a moment of false ease. What were those dark cars doing outside my building? Who were those guys? Why were Joe and I shot at, and where was Joe? I was also wondering if the police could hear the bus announcements over the P.A.

when I placed the call to them. It doesn't matter now. I'm gone.

Several hours later the bus dropped me about ten miles from Rob's house. He was so surprised to hear from me, he came right over to pick me up. On the ride home I told him all that had transpired, he seemed more puzzled than me, but was a calming ally in a night of sheer terror. He suggested I call the cops again in the morning. And, suggested that I do so from a pay phone, not his house phone.

I thought he was being overly cautious, but it's his home, his rules.

Tara, when I called the police, they didn't even have my previous call listed in any report. The desk sergeant started asking me a lot of questions. I answered them as best I could with all this fear creeping again into my mind. I told him about not being able to reach Joe. He asked me where I was, but I refused to answer and hung up. Rob and I were totally puzzled. The next day I called again, and this time the dispatcher acknowledged my call from the day before. I was told they dispatched a car to the Trade Center, yet no one knew anything about shots being fired. I told the guy there were crates and crates of explosives stacked in the hallway. Did they check on the crates? "Nothing was found to my knowledge, sir." Tara, they were there, I wasn't dreaming! Could they have moved them somewhere else? Sure they could have, but was anything checked out at all? I don't know, and was glad I had chosen to flee. The dispatcher said I should come to the station and file a report. I hung up the phone.

Then I thought I would try to get a hold of Joe again, with the awful fear of what had maybe happened to him haunting me. I called, hoping beyond hope that I would hear his voice with some relieving answer to all of this insanity. He didn't answer his cell phone. I tried his home phone. His Mom answered. As soon as she heard it was me, she said she had thought of calling me, but Joe had told her I wasn't working at the Trade Centers anymore. It seemed Joe hadn't been home for a couple of days, he hasn't shown up at work, and no one has seen him for days. At the time of my conversation with his mother, it had been THREE days! The poor woman filed a missing persons report on him after waiting the requisite 24 hours, and ever since has been calling the hospitals. My heart sank to the floor. And, my mind froze. I wound up not telling her anything about that night. Maybe it's cowardly, maybe it was fear, and maybe it was the heartbreak of having to deal with the aftermath of feeling as if I should have stuck around to find out what happened to him. I just couldn't find the words to tell her what happened that night. Forgive me, Tara, I just didn't have the nerve and my thoughts were all jumbled talking to her and finding out he never made it home...

I told Mrs. Grabowski I would let her know if I heard from him and not to worry. Yes, I felt like the ultimate fraud, and with my heart broken, we hung up. I am at a loss and really just don't know what to think. Right now my mind is set to 'survival.' My own survival!

What is going on??

Rob's been questioning me quite extensively. When I told him about a rumor which had been circulating, he commented that now everything made sense.

Before I was laid off, the rumor in the Towers was that a high premium terrorist clause was put into the insurance policy. Rob thinks this rumor, coupled with the crates of explosives, has something to do with insurance fraud. What? Rob said he wasn't sure, but couldn't come up with another scenario that made sense. He reasons that given the Towers are a key target for terrorists, a little explosion here and there could make it look like it was a terrorist attack. He may be onto something, but I'm still racking my brain to see if another reason is staring us in the face.

I have moments of wishful thinking that this will just blow over but I have doubts. From being shot at, from the ominous pick-up call from Joe's cell phone, to those men at my apartment, to now my apartment being ransacked? Now you can really understand why I am in the state I'm in. How I worry about every possible link between us or anyone finding out I'm in Maine.

Where is Joe? What happened to him? Was it the new security that shot at us? When I was a guard at the Towers we would have never shot at anyone unless it was a life or death matter. And we never did. Even when a knife-wielding deranged individual came into the lobby one day, wondering where his money had gone.

Tara, how I wish we were still at the Hamptons, wandering the beach in search of those sea glass gems and colorful shells. Pretending we were two survivors after a shipwreck. Nothing to do but start a new life together. Secretly hoping we would never be rescued. I guess you could say what has come to pass here is like the shipwreck, only you're not here with me. Except at the tip of my pen as I reach out to you. I should have been a writer instead of a security guard. You make it so easy for me to create such scenarios.

Now I need to know that you are safe. The fact that there is no telephone here adds to the feel of isolation. And yes, again and again, I should have listened to you when you told me to get a cell phone when I had to turn mine in to the company! It's good that there is that payphone not too far from here. I feel like one day soon we'll be saying, "Payphones — remember those things?" They are getting so hard to find.

I still can't believe Rutherford is missing. What he might be going through if he is wandering the streets of New York City. I have had him since he was just a kitten, and that is the only home he has known. It really diminishes what valuables might be missing. I want to believe it was just what the police suspect. Some kids looking to hang out, and a half stocked refrigerator to raid. But given all I know, it's very possible those men got into my apartment that night.

I so appreciate you keeping an eye out for Rutherford. I know it's a long shot that he might return, but he is too proud to be at the mercy of the NYC streets. In case those men are watching the place, please be extremely careful. In fact, maybe it's best if you don't go back to my place. Oh God, Tara, I'm not sure if I'm blowing this out of proportion, or if being cautious is what is needed right now.

I have been chopping wood during the daytime to sort of earn my keep. And when Rob is here we go night fishing a lot. It is great pulling in those bass at night. The very bright moonlight gives the only view of the excitement. After so many years in the city, I think I could get used to this kind of life for awhile. I'm aching from chopping, and aching for you…

I remember how time stood still when I held you in my arms. Now I feel like time is standing still again as I wait to hold you once again. The stillness of this place, which is a big part of its beauty, is a stark contrast to the anxiety I feel here alone. The stillness of the night serves no distraction to my missing you. I want to come and nestle with you under the covers. I want to do all those things we loved, under the covers. I am okay Tara. Nobody but Rob knows where I am.

I can't believe how long this letter is! Guess I needed to get a lot off my chest and with all this time on my hands…

OX

Blake

P.S. Oh before I forget, could you see if my address book is still in the apartment when you go back? It is in the second drawer down of my desk on the right.

"Jerry's Pigeons are above us all"

— Genya Ravan

Blake,

No sooner had I finished your letter did I start this one. You're scaring me Blake. I'm unraveled.

Your letter has me frightened. I can't believe you were shot at! Shot at! By the new security team? That's crazy! No wonder you left so quickly. I knew you were chased, but now knowing you were shot at — it makes sense why you think your apartment may not have been a standard ole' NYC break-in.

And Joe? What do you think happened to Joe? Oh my God, what if he was shot, Blake? Well, of course you've considered this. Perhaps he's hiding out, just like you are doing in Maine. Have you tried reaching out to the police again?

I understand why you didn't tell Joe's mom what happened. At first. But surely you see how important it is to let her know what transpired that night. At the very least her missing person's report coupled with your report of you and Joe being shot at, matters.

Look, I can understand your initial reticence about letting Mrs. Grabowski know. You weren't supposed to be there, you were frightened out of your wits (understatement) and without absolute knowledge of what happened to Joe, what exactly could you tell her? Yet you have to call her back and yes, Blake, ultimately the police are going to want to talk to you. At least they have an account of your previous call so they won't wonder why you didn't come forward earlier — you DID come forward!

If you haven't already done so, you need to call Mrs. Grabowski, Blake. If Joe still hasn't returned she must be going out of her mind. Literally out of her mind. You need to call her back.

I'm a little confused on Rob's rationale regarding insurance fraud. It seems like a huge leap. Are you implying that those explosives are going to be set off to collect insurance? To make it look like terrorists did it so insurance can be collected? I agree with you, this seems like a HUGE leap.

If indeed this is what is happening, do you think this can wait until your return? I know you're coming back next week, but this doesn't seem to be something that should wait a week. Call someone! I think you have a responsibility to do so.

Tomorrow I will check for your address book. Hope you don't mind, but when I go over to your place, Carol and Suzanne are going to join me. Since being with you, I haven't seen my friends in a while! They've been wondering about this mystery man, and why I've dropped out of doing anything with them. It'll be good to have them along so in case anything looks suspicious, or ANYONE looks suspicious, I'm not alone. Anyway, Carol, Suzanne and I are going to see "Along Came a Spider" which should be good. We're going to see it at the Bijou, which is right down the street from your apartment. So again, hope you don't mind that they're joining me. Truthfully? There's another reason to stop by your place — brace yourself —

Rutherford is back!

Yesterday, as soon as I opened the door he was sitting on the back of your couch. Of course when he realized it was me he jumped down and hid under the sofa. Mrs. Ward told me she found him in the lobby the night before. She put him in your place with a plate of tuna. I thought about coming back to feed him like I originally planned, but have to admit to being a little spooked ever since your place was burglarized. So, I've decided to bring Rutherford back to my place. Truth be told, I'm glad I made that decision given all that you wrote in your last letter. Hope this is okay with you. I know Rutherford isn't going to like it! I know he's going to flip out, but I don't feel comfortable going to your place every day. I hope you understand and that Rutherford forgives me. Suzanne and Carol are going to help get him in the crate and carry all his food and toys back here. Hopefully with three of us working to get him in his carryall he won't have a choice.

I should also tell you that IRS agents looking for you visited Mrs. Ward. Since she had problems with the IRS six years ago, she told them to get off her property. She can get really feisty! Anyway, thought you should know there are two IRS agents looking for you. I'm sure this isn't welcomed news after having been laid off from your job, been shot at, don't know where Joe is, your apartment has been burglarized, and well, this couldn't have come at a worse time.

Which, by the way, I'm sure you're going to think these IRS agents might be those guys who you saw at your apartment jimmying your lock, but Mrs. Ward assured me they were IRS agents.

Please call me soon. It's hard waiting days for your reply, and your last letter really has me concerned. I really, really think you need to go to the authorities and yes, call Mrs. Grabowski.

XOXO (Why do you write "OX"? Is that because you don't mean "hugs and kisses?")

T

P.S. I wasn't able to locate your address book. Could it be somewhere else?

"The real hero is always a hero by mistake; he dreams of being an honest coward like everybody else"

— Umbert Eco

———◆———

My sweet lady,

I did try Joe's mom again and the poor woman is going out of her mind. Joe hasn't returned. Oh Tara, this surely means Joe is dead. I feel just horrible. There was a part of me that wanted to believe he'd get on the phone and we'd laugh about our adventure. That I would return home and everything would be back to normal with me looking for a job and you and I continuing where we left off. Sadly, I'm not sure this is going to happen now. With Joe missing since that night? Tara, this can only mean one thing. He was hit by their bullets and is likely dead. At best, he could be injured. Again, I didn't have the heart to tell his mother what happened that night. It dawned on me that when I told the police what happened that evening, I told them I couldn't find my friend Joe. They have his name. Why aren't they matching up Mrs. Grabowski's missing person's report with my account of shots fired at the Towers? I'm sorry Tara, you are bound to think I'm a coward and maybe you're right, but I just couldn't tell Mrs. Grabowski what happened. I didn't want to explain why I didn't go to the police straight away. Why did I call instead of going to the police station? Why did I hop a bus to Maine? I have to admit I wonder that myself sometimes. I was just so frightened when Joe didn't wind up at Sullivans for that beer. When I called his cell and someone picked up, but wouldn't answer? Then those guys at my apartment? My only thought was 'flight.' How could I tell Mrs. Grabowski that this was my first thought when I wasn't sure if one of those bullets hit her son? I'm agonizing over this situation, but don't see now how I can go back and tell her anything.

Now there are IRS agents looking for me? Believe me, Tara, there is no way I owe the IRS anything and why would they talk to Mrs. Ward? Suspiciously *after* I get shot at, *after* men are seen at my apartment door. *Coincidentally* after my apartment is ransacked and now that I know Joe never returned that evening? Those guys, if indeed they were with the new security personnel they installed, could have looked up Joe and my employee record. I'm sure no less than 50 cameras caught our image in the Towers that night. It'd be easy to find out who we are in just a matter of minutes. Did the newly installed security guards run down my information and seek me out? Are they protecting an insurance fraud scandal? If indeed that's how those crates of explosives are going to be used? Will I be safe when I return to my apartment? To the city? I don't have anything pressing right now so maybe I should wait a bit longer before returning. I'm in total flux. I've got to get off this subject before I go crazy.

It's too good to be true that Rutherford has returned. I really doubted I would ever see him again.

But I am so thankful…and to Mrs. Ward for spotting him. I never thought he could make it out on the streets. I even hoped somebody had him. But he survived, and quite well I guess. He's Rugged Rutherford and I am proud of him.

I don't want you going back to my place, ever. I'm terribly frightened Tara and I'm just grateful no one really knows about you in my life. I want to keep you safe and it's agonizing knowing there's little I can do so far away. Suffice it to say don't go back to my apartment. Okay?

After talking to Mrs. Grabowski, I called my mom. She doesn't know I was laid off from the Towers. I didn't want to worry her and figured once I got a new job I'd just tell her the bad/good news at one time. She is so sweet and anxious to meet you Tara! She wants to know that you are good enough for her Blake. That's a laugh, if you're good enough. I can't believe I'm good enough for you. Anyway it appears we are just "so good" for each other.

The reason I write OX at the end of my letters is just to contrast your XO…and I wanted to see if you would notice the difference. You did!

OX

Blake

"Fear is the parent of cruelty"

— James Anthony Froude

Blake,

I wish you would call so we could talk about everything instead of writing these long letters. I do understand why you're not willing to talk on a public payphone. Surely there are times when you can call me at night when few people are around. I left a message on Rob's answering machine asking you to call me. I know he's at his house and you're at one of the cabins, but assume the two of you get together every couple of days. I mean, how else are my letters reaching you? Am I right?

From the sounds of it, it seems as if you're thinking of spending more time up in Maine. I could be misreading your latest letter (again the reason why phone conversations are MUCH better!), but that's how I'm reading it.

Blake, I'm frightened for you. You were shot at and one of your best friends is missing. The issue I have is why you aren't still trying the authorities? Why don't you call and ask to speak to a sergeant or someone like that. If they follow through on your information, this would certainly give more weight to Mrs. Grabowski's missing person's report and a formal investigation can be launched. Especially now that they have you listed as making a few phone calls. Then there's the report of your apartment being broken into — there's a definitive thread of questionable activity that lends more credence to your account of what happened that night at the Towers.

Why not call the insurance company? If you really feel insurance fraud is being perpetrated, contact the Towers insurance company and have them launch an investigation. Something needs to be done Blake and I'm not sure this can wait until you return.

Sitting up in Maine hoping things will go away isn't going to get you anywhere. So what if you went back to the Towers to pick up stuff in your locker? I think the fact that you and Joe saw those explosives AND were shot at is much more important information than an ex-security guard entered the building to pick up stuff he left behind.

Consider what Mrs. Grabowski is going through. The poor woman is racked with questions about her son's disappearance and you have information.

Please. Think about what I'm saying here, okay?

The fact that Joe never made it home that night does NOT mean he is dead. I'll grant you that this is a possibility, but Blake, seriously...don't even go there. Joe could be holed up like you are in a secure location. It's not as if he'd walk back into the office the next day regaling co-workers with his tale of being shot at the night before. He too might be figuring out what to do. Have you tried his cell phone again?

Look, I know why you want to keep your whereabouts secret and can't imagine how scary this has been for you. I just think....well I've already stated what I think. I'll save the rest of my comments for when you return.

Rutherford is now with me and is not happy about it. I found his carrier with no problem. As suspected, as soon as he saw the carrier he bolted. Once Suzanne, Carol and I wrestled him into it he meowed all the way back to my place. You should have seen the stares I got on the subway! Then when I got him home and let him out? He bolted under the couch. Although I haven't been able to locate him (he's no longer under the couch), don't worry he's not missing! His food is being eaten and litter box needs tending every day so I know he's around…he's just making himself scarce. It's apparently going to take him a little time to warm up to me.

I hate to mention this, but when we went to pick up Rutherford, Mrs. Ward told me those IRS agents returned asking questions about you and wondering if she had any information on where they might be able to locate you. As before, she didn't tell them anything. What could she tell them? I did find out they flashed their credentials, so Blake, I do think they are legitimate IRS agents.

Please think about coming back soon. In addition to squaring everything with Mrs. Grabowski and the police, it'll be so good to be held in your arms once again. To look into those deep hazel eyes and see the man I fell for two months ago in that Starbucks. I feel as though we just started and I don't want to spend another day, another hour, another minute apart. Please, come home.

xo

Tara

"Conscience is the inner voice that
warns us somebody may be looking"

— H.L. Menchken

———◆———

Dear Sweet Tara,

Wow, I've written four letters to you in a little under three weeks! That's a record! Granted, being in this cabin gives me plenty of time to pound these letters out. Time certainly has a different pace here.

I've been giving some thought to your suggestion to call the NYC police department again. I was actually thinking since explosives are involved perhaps I should let the FBI know. Or that group — ATF I think it's called. I just don't know yet.

What I can tell you is that although I extended my stay another week it's not only because I'm apprehensive about coming back to the city, but it's been four years since I've had a vacation. I figure once I'm back in the city I can deal with all this mess. Right now I'm just trying to enjoy myself while figuring out what I should do upon my return. I do have to say that it'd be better with you here beside me. I too miss "us."

I know it's not a good light I'm shining on myself here, but I don't want to think about what happened to Joe and I don't want to think about what those crates of explosives mean. I don't want to pretend that I don't see a connection with my apartment being broken into or the implication of IRS agents showing up looking for me. TWICE? I can't pretend none of these things have an evil thread of danger attached to it all.

Like the fact you couldn't find my address book? That has an ominous feel to it. It was surely in my desk drawer and while I know my place was ransacked, you and Mrs. Ward would have come upon it. Did these guys get my phone book and now are systematically going through it, looking for me? Thankfully you are not in my address book. As soon as you gave me your number I memorized it!

Right now, I just want to sit back, fish with Rob, take walks in the woods and enjoy the beauty of this state. I'm sure to be back on a bus to the city soon, so don't worry my love, I will come back and make everything right. With Joe, with Mrs. Grabowski and with you.

I can't wait to see you again. Watch you run to my arms. Look into those eyes that captured me. Feel the woman I have waited for all my life, warm against my body. I can still taste your kiss from memory. Oh Tara, I know it hasn't been, but it seems so long since you were next to me. When I return I will find a way to keep you next to me, endlessly.

I am aching for your touch again. It's all frosting on the cake of love~~~

OX

Blake

"A friendship that like love is warm;
A love like friendship, steady"

— Thomas Moore

Dear, Sweet Blake,

I'm so glad we had a chance to talk last night. Talking about our trip to the Hamptons has created a film reel in my head, playing back scenes of our time together. The look in your eyes, the feel of your hand lightly placed on the small of my back, the cow that refused to move for us, your inventive means of getting the cow to move(!), the feel of you beside me in bed, the way the moon shone through the kitchen window when we were doing the dishes, and our conversation about nature, life, our shared philosophies...

our sharing of everything sacred and precious.

How is it possible that someone with the same sensibilities, cares, concerns and thoughts as my own exists? What are the odds of meeting in a coffee shop of all places?

And with each discovery, with each moment we spend together, our lives intertwine more.

In your presence.

in your care,

as you, my dear sweet man are

in my care.

Is it possible anything this good could last forever? I've never felt this way toward another, Blake. Never. It's as if my very existence now hinges on our being together.

I know you feel the same way.

Yet here we are,

the beat of our hearts finding the same rhythm, while miles separate us.

I know how scared you are and why you're scared. I also respected your wishes not to talk last night about any of the stuff that has been going on, but please Blake. Were you to come home and talk to the authorities I promise you someone would take what you saw in the Towers that night seriously.

I thought of something else. What if I went to the insurance company? Surely they would be interested in a potential fraud case. Do you remember the name of the insurance company? You wouldn't have to be involved at all. I could discreetly reach out to them. In fact, I could call them from a pay phone and without revealing my name, tell them just enough to pique their interest and check it out. If this is indeed insurance fraud as we think, by exposing what is going on, no longer would those guys be interested in what you saw — they'd be found out!

What do you think of this idea?

I know this is an unashamed attempt to get you back here to the city, back here with me, but can you blame me?

Your fears are valid, Blake. I'm just worried. You not only extended your vacation two weeks, you told me last night that you're going to be there until mid-September!

Thank you for inviting me to visit you in Maine over the long weekend, but after careful consideration I feel I really need to spend the weekend at my aunt's Labor Day party. It's an annual family event and the only time I get to see my extended family. I was REALLY hoping you would be back to join me (whimper, whimper). You can stay here with me. As you said, no one knows of my connection to you and to this end wouldn't be able to find you here.

I can't go back, Blake. I can't go back to the life I had before meeting you. I just can't.

It's as if you "woke" me up and I can't go back to the time before "you." I want to be with you. I hate that you're scared. I understand it, but hate it and wish there was an easy solution to all this. Maybe the IRS guys are IRS guys. Maybe, well....I can't explain the actions of the guys who shot at you. There is no explanation.

I've enclosed some money for you. I wish it were more.

Come back to the city, Blake.

In the absence of you, my heart is breaking.

xo

Tara

"Love isn't there to make us happy. I believe it
exists to show us how much we can endure"

— Hermann Hesse

Tara,

After reading the letter you just sent me, your descriptions dance around my heart like children singing. I have loved being here in Maine, with all its rustic beauty. But now it feels like a hideaway, till we meet again. I know what you mean about our existence hinging on our being together. I have always felt quite self-sufficient and confident to be alone. Now that confidence has lost its meaning, and there's a new definition of sufficient that requires you...

If I didn't have you, I truly can't imagine holding up under the circumstances. I really want to come back to the city and share what I have seen with the authorities and Mrs. Grabowski. I know you want me to return and the thought of us being together again is beyond alluring. I will return, Tara. Soon. That is my promise to you.

I've been missing you, Tara. This past weekend was particularly hard. Maybe it's the fact I haven't seen you now in four weeks! Why by the time you receive this letter I'll be days away from holding you in my arms.

Next year? I'm there front and center at your family's Labor Day party.

I can't remember the name of the insurance company. So I don't have a name to readily contact for a potential fraud case. I know that could be remedied, but again I want no trail that leads to you. So while I thank you for your kind offer, I'm not going to ask you to call on my behalf. I'll deal with all of this when I return.

Get this! After talking to you the other night I called my mom who told me SHE HAD BEEN VISITED BY IRS agents looking for me! Why would two IRS agents go all the way to Ohio? Now there is reason to think they represent my worst fears. Now do you see why I wanted to stay up here just a little longer before coming back?

I'm thankful to think of Rutherford being there with you. Even if he hasn't warmed up to you yet, just give him time. Again, I don't want you going to my place anymore for any reason. Mrs. Ward can keep an eye on it for me. And thank you for sending money. As we discussed, I don't feel comfortable taking money out of my account or writing any checks. I know this seems incredibly paranoid, but I'm taking extra precautions until I get back to the city and straighten everything out. I did call Mrs. Ward and told her I'd be late with September's rent. She was more concerned about the IRS agents. I told her there was no problem with my taxes.

I will pay you back, my sweet angel.

OX,

Blake

"Fighting terrorism is like being a goalkeeper. You can make a hundred brilliant saves but the only shot that people remember is the one that gets past you"

— Paul Wilkinson

Blake,

Even though we just talked yesterday, I had to write down my experiences. It's surreal what is happening here. You would no longer recognize NY. People are walking around dumbfounded, dazed, uncertainty in their eyes. The streets are eerily empty of cars and every time an ambulance or police car blasts down the street, everyone looks up. Some with cautious anticipation, some with desperation written all over their face. Does the ambulance carry a loved one? Is there another attack taking place?

We are the walking wounded.

September 11, 2001, will long be a remembered date.

A fine layer of ash coats the streets and buildings and everywhere I step a soft cloud kicks up. The authorities tell us not to go outside, not to expose ourselves to the air until they give the all-clear signal, but if a family member or friend is missing, how is it not possible to walk the streets in search of them? Ever since I heard Carol was in the Towers, I've been looking for her. I know you don't know Carol, but trust me....for her to switch shifts to work early morning — unheard of. Carol would sleep till noon every day if she could so the fact that this one day she does a friend a favor? Well, that's just the person she was Blake. Scratch that — that's the person she IS. I refuse to use the past tense when speaking of her.

Evidently, she started work at 7:30 and when the first plane hit, she ran. That's all I know. My heart breaks thinking of how terrified she must have been. Carol and I have known each other since kindergarten and have told each other literally everything, since we first pinky swore we'd be best friends forever. All growing up she would be at my house sleeping over, or I'd be at her house. We were inseparable.

I spent the morning with her mother taping up pictures of Carol everywhere. Yesterday we hit the hospitals and are thinking of going back to some of them tonight. My phone still works, but Mrs. Willard's phone is out and when I suggested we make calls from here, she refused. She prefers instead to go to the hospitals just in case there are people being treated who are unidentified. It's apparent she needs to be out looking for Carol. I understand. We put Carol's picture up everywhere, pretty much covering the perimeter of the Towers, but clearly we weren't able to get too close. The officials aren't letting anyone near the site. Carol's mom brought along masks so we wouldn't be exposed to the foul air and Blake, it is foul. I can't describe the smell, but can tell you that when I got home this afternoon I took an hour-long shower and still that sickening smell is trapped in my nose. I know this sounds crazy, but I can still feel it on my skin. Like it's alive and undulating beneath the surface.

Even though I wish you were here, no one should be exposed to this horror. I'm still having a hard time coming to grips with it all. How can humans harbor such hatred and how is it possible 19 men were able to find in each other this shared hatred for America? All those people on the airplanes... can you imagine being told to call your loved ones right before you die? And what of those passengers in Pennsylvania? Courageous souls, all of them. To be confronted by evil and still be able to find the power to rise up and take a stand...unbelievable.

That word fits nicely for everything going on. Unbelievable.

I don't want to write of this horrible tragedy only Blake, for I'm sure even in that little rustic cabin you're getting plenty of information from the news channels. Here it's on 24 hours a day with different pundits and experts trying to explain what happened. I sit watching, but not watching. Dazed, confused, heartbroken. The only time I pay attention is when they show the list of people missing. They'll show a picture of the person missing along with their name. I sit riveted seeing all those faces, wondering if the next one they show is someone I know. Hopeful with each image that the person is safe.

I never thought I'd say this, but it was a blessing they laid you off. How weird life's twists and turns are when we reflect back on our storyline and see how and why things happened. Then again, we never really do know the whys and wherefores of anything, do we Blake?

Just a short while ago, you were devastated about losing your job, certain insurance fraud was being perpetrated at the Towers, and today you're safely up in Maine. As night falls outside my window and a sliver of moon hangs behind fast-moving clouds, I just want to shut my eyes and envision being with you in Maine. Away from here.

My mom called twice today trying to convince me to come home, get out of the city. She never did like the idea of me moving to New York and right now I'm thinking she's right. Maybe I never should have come here.

Then I remind myself that if I hadn't come here, I wouldn't have met you.

But you aren't here, Blake, and I'm so lonely and so frightened. I'm sorry to be so "needy," but I'm overwhelmed with sorrow. The art gallery is closed for the week. Obviously at a time like this, no one is considering what to put on their walls and Christos and Cassy lost loved ones.

I'm serving breakfast down at Willy's for the workers. While everyone is trying to keep spirits up, it's hard to render a smile when the faces of the workers are filled with desperation and despair. We are a broken people, Blake.

Were you able to reach George and/or Justin? I hope everyone is all right. I feel as if I know your friends from some of the stories you've shared about them. If there is anything I can do — contact them, seek out family members — just let me know. How hard it must be to watch all this unfold on TV and not be here with your friends. Obviously, they aren't letting anyone back in the city. Not yet, so your extended vacation just got extended a bit more.

I've enclosed a phone card for you. There's $30 on it which I hope gives you enough minutes. Don't worry about paying me back. The phone company was handing these cards out down at Willy's.

Ah Blake, I wish I had better news to share. If you get a chance, could you try and call me again this week? It's frustrating not having a number where I can call you. I'm so afraid and so lonely. I sit here in my apartment with the lights off and still the lights from the rescue efforts are so bright, it's a constant reminder of Tuesday morning when the world seemed to stop and evil found an opening.

I guess now all our conversations about insurance fraud seem silly. And if there was any intention to exact insurance fraud? The terrorists readily took care of the problem with several planes, determination and hatred.

Come home, Blake. Not just yet…not until things get back to some semblance of normalcy here in the city, but please come home to me. I've never felt so alone.

xo

Tara

"The big threat to America is the way
we react to terrorism by throwing
away what everybody values about our
country — a commitment to human
rights. America is a great nation because
we are a good nation. When we stop being
a good nation, we stop being great"

— Bobby Kennedy

——◆——

Tara, My Love,

It seems we are caught up in all of the heartbreaking loss, even though we have no personal family members missing. I'm so sorry to hear Carol is missing. And so glad her mother has you to help her through this, the hardest part of her life. I'm pulling for you, as I know this is so difficult. How can this be happening?

It occurred to me that Joe's missing person's report might get lost in the sea of what must be countless missing people reports. This saddens me greatly.

I was able to contact a friend of mine who was in the subbasement minutes before the Towers collapsed. Did you hear there were explosions down in the subbasement? Some guys were seriously injured from the blast. I only heard about this from talking to Juan. I didn't hear anything about it on the news. But I have missed a lot. Why would there be explosions in the subbasement when the plane hit eighty floors above?

I saw the story about the plane that went down in Shanksville, PA. I can't believe the only thing left is a crater. The plane must have hit the ground so hard there was nearly nothing left. Those poor people had several moments to realize their fate was clearly at hand. I can't imagine the feeling. Yet was surprised there was little plane wreckage.

Rob reminded me that Americans are not used to having horror at their doorstep. It is always overseas somewhere, and out of the realm of our reality. We have always been so safe for the most part.

I hate to think of you there crying about it all, when I can't help you or hold you. Our new love is being tested without us really even knowing it. It is the knowledge that you are there, and I am here, that gives us something to hold on to in the face of such loss. If not for each other where would we be Tara? I'm so thankful for you, my unexpected dream come true, as you keep me sane in the middle of a nightmare.

I've been watching the walking wounded on the constant TV footage of the aftermath in the city. If people weren't chased down the street or buried by the plumes of dust and debris, they are so heavy at heart trying not to accept that in all likelihood their father, mother, sister, brother, has perished in this horror.

I've been trying to imagine what the awful smell you speak of in the air is. I do know that there was a lot of asbestos in those Towers. If you are waiting for an all clear from the authorities about the air quality, I would still think twice about breathing in much of it.

I am almost afraid to see what they have done to the greatest city on Earth. When I return it will be like returning home to survey the homeland after a war. I have seen so many pictures and videos of the devastation, it's like I already know what I will behold. But to see it in person will be exceedingly horrible. While finding you in my eyes will bring a sweet relief for me, so many people can't hope to expect at this point. Still, I just can't wait to see you Tara.

If I may find some sanity in your description of all this, it is unbelievable. It is hard for us to grasp the meaning of things revealed, at least until we have some foresight in hindsight. I suppose I was lucky to be laid off when I was. Though at the time I sure didn't think so…till I met you. Now there is even more reason to feel blessed. I may have very well been inside those buildings helping out or aiding someone. I can't imagine the brief horror some experienced when they realized the building was coming down on them.

Yes, you would have never met me without venturing to the Big Apple, and I would have never met you without being laid off. The fates have had us in play these many weeks for sure. I don't know what it all means but I do know that I am lucky beyond belief. So thankful to have you. And even though I don't have you at my side, so grateful you are safe.

All my love,

OX,

Blake

"Terrorism has become the systematic
weapon of a war that knows no
borders or seldom has a face"

— Jacques Chirac

Dear, Sweet Blake,

I've enclosed another $300 for you and another phone card. I'm sorry this letter is so short, but I'm just now getting home after working at Willy's for twelve hours and putting up Carol's picture with her mom for two hours. I'm just beat.

Sweet dreams, my love.

Tara

"Nobody ever sees truth
except in fragments"

— Henry Ward Beecher

—◆—

Tara,

I hate to think of you there in the city feeling alone. And I feel more than alone here in Maine. Helpless, as this insane parade of information intrudes into every corner of my mind. How strange what I saw in the Towers that night that led me to fear an insurance fraud possibility.

Rob had me go down to the library with him to watch footage of the cloud of debris that chased people down the streets of New York, after the Towers fell. I've seen this footage a hundred times. What gives? He's been making me do a lot of "homework" lately. Sometimes I wish he would just tell me what these things are, but he wants me to look into things with a critical eye and not blindly believe everything he tells me. Feeling like a kid whose been told by his dad to go do his homework, we logged onto the computer and watched the horror unfold as people ran down the streets with that big cloud of dust barreling down on them.

He then had me look up pyroclastic clouds. Interesting. The footage of these rolling clouds with an infinite amount of debris, looked just like what happened on 9/11. So?

So get this...the ONLY TWO SCENARIOS WHEN PYROCLASTIC CLOUDS APPEAR ARE EITHER VOLCANIC ERUPTION OR DEMOLITION. What? I told him it's not possible. He then had me watch footage of collapsed buildings. No pyroclastic cloud. Then I watched a building being demolished. Pyroclastic cloud.

Rob asked if I noted anything else peculiar. I was so stunned by what I had already seen I didn't know what he was talking about. He made me pay close attention to how a building collapses. We must have looked at 10 examples. Then he showed me examples of buildings that are demolition. I saw where he was going straightaway, but he had me look at the Towers coming down again. A scene I've watched on the news a million times, but not until he pointed it out, did I get it. The Towers did not collapse. They were demolition. Look how they came down in their own footprint. Demolition. There is NO WAY anyone can look at the footage for both scenarios and walk away thinking the buildings collapsed. No way!

As if that wasn't enough, Rob then had me look at the properties of jet fuel and how hot it must be for steel to melt. Again, feeling as if I've been issued my homework assignment, I checked into it and was surprised to learn that jet fuel is basically kerosene and could never reach a temperature high enough to melt steel.

Steel starts to weaken at 1,270 degrees and MELTS at 2,800 degrees.

Kerosene in open-air burns at 575 degrees.

Steel melts at 2,800 degrees and kerosene, at its hottest, burns at 575 degrees. Now it makes sense to me how all those people were standing at the window waving for help. If we buy into the official story about the steel melting, wouldn't it be too hot by the windows?

What Rob is telling me is true. At least the research bears this out. The buildings were demolitioned (is that even a word?). I saw the planes go in, heard the explanation of how and why the Towers came down, but have to agree with Rob — this isn't adding up.

Look how the Towers came down in their own footprint and then watch the pyroclastic cloud come down the street. Now add in the crates of explosives I saw almost one month to the day of the "attack!"

DEMOLITION.

What really got me thinking was Juan's account of explosions in the subbasement. I immediately called George, who, as you know, I've been trying to reach. I was finally able to catch him at home. He confirmed Juan's account of the explosions in the subbasement, and he himself, was pretty badly hurt. He recently got out of the hospital, which is the reason I hadn't been able to reach him earlier. He told me many of my former co-workers, whose offices were in the subbasement, were seriously injured and he heard some even perished. How does a plane eighty floors up cause damage in the basement? From what I can gather, it wasn't the collapse of the buildings that wreaked havoc down there. According to George, people were being evacuated with injuries before the plane even hit! I can't wrap my head around this one. Then again, when we talked George was heavily medicated so maybe he's misremembering. Still, he and Juan both say there was an explosion in the subbasement.

I really wish you had been able to find my address book so I could call more of my friends. As it is, I just remember Joe, Juan, George and Justin's numbers. I'm still trying to reach Justin. I hope he's ok. Like many I know who worked there, you have to wonder.

This is all pretty scary stuff, Tara, yet I know it pales in comparison to your personal tragedy. Again, I am so sorry to hear about your best friend Carol. I am praying she has turned up. Your heart will be broken beyond repair if she hasn't. Her mother must be scared to death — a parent's worst possible fear. What else can she do but keep looking?

I have to admit to being encouraged that so many people want to help out at what they are calling "Ground Zero." The residents of NY usually seem so isolated from one another, it is good to see them pulling together.

Thank you for the phone card. I will call you in the morning when I go into town. Obviously, our call will have happened by the time you read this, but then again I plan on calling you as often as possible to make sure you're okay. I plan to also try Justin again.

I think of you often, Tara, and hold you safe in my heart. I ache for what you and Mrs. Willard are going through looking for Carol. Wish I were there, but given "IRS" agents are looking for me…given those men probably want to shut me up, given the crates of explosives I saw…it's not safe for me.

OX

Blake

"It is the peculiar nature of the world
to go on spinning no matter what
sort of heartbreak is happening"

— Sue Monk Kidd

My darling Blake,

How I wish everyone was safe and life was like it was on September 10th. Carol is still among the missing. Her mom, Suzanne and I spend most of our days making rounds to the hospitals, making sure there isn't a new admission who hasn't been identified; ensuring the flyers we put up are still there and trying to locate her co-workers to see if they know anything.

Thankfully the gallery is still closed. Wow, it's been almost a month now. Even still, I don't think I can go back to work any time soon.

The longer Carol is missing, the more apparent it is that she is probably not going to be found. I dare not say these words to Carol's mother. Mrs. Willard is probably thinking the same thing, but we have to remain hopeful.

I remember once when we were sixteen Carol and I were dating some "bad" boys. I like to think wanting the "bad" boy is a phase every teenage girl goes through, so please no comments! This one particular night we're riding around in my boyfriend's 4x4 with Carol and her boyfriend, Matt, in the back. All of a sudden there are two cop cars behind us with their lights flashing. Since we were on this little back road, it was apparent they were stopping us, but my boyfriend, Rory, decided to gun it. Off we go topping 90 mph with Carol and I screaming to stop and Matt encouraging Rory on, "pedal to the metal, bro." With barely a chance to register what was happening, the truck suddenly takes a sharp right turn and we find ourselves on a golf course. I'm screaming that I'm going to open the door and jump out, and Rory reaches over and takes my hand just as calm as can be as the truck dips down into a sand trap, spraying white sand up over the hood and all along the sides. I'm surprised we didn't get stuck right there, but the truck kept going and so did the cops. There were now three cop cars behind us! As soon as we hit the 17th green (I know it was the 17th green from the little flag), there were three other cop cars sitting there waiting for us. It was over. Rory did a 180 on the green with the truck coming to a shuddering stop. Six cop cars surrounded the 17th green. Surrounded us! With a bullhorn, the cops told us to get out of the truck with our hands raised, first instructing Rory to kill the engine and drop the keys out the window. He tosses the keys far from the truck like a stupid-o thinking he's making it harder on the cops. He's got quite an attitude and is yelling and cursing at them. Carol and I are lying side-by-side on the green with fingertips touching. She has her head turned to the right and mine is turned to the left. I'm drawing comfort from her and though in hindsight it's not as if WE broke the law, yet for a sixteen-year-old honors student, this is a tragic event. What will I tell my parents? How am I going to make that phone call home? Within fifteen minutes we're being interviewed separately. Seems Rory is a well-known drug dealer and the cops were making a routine stop to see if he had any drugs in the truck. I didn't even know he took drugs. Another ten minutes and I'm frantic thinking any minute they are going to handcuff, then put us in the back of the cop car and take us downtown to "book" us. One of the cops comes over and tells me I'm lucky to have such a good cousin. I'm confused, cousin? Fortunately I was paralyzed with fear and didn't open my mouth because the next thing I know the cops are acting all nice and kindly put Carol and me in the back of a cop car without handcuffs. Seems Carol told them we were out on a date with these guys, but didn't realize they were "druggies." Since she comes from a prominent family, some of the cops knew her dad. They decided to let her walk, telling her they didn't want her dad to find out where she was or who she was with, "Your father, he's a good man and would be deeply disappointed in you!" she was told over and over again. They weren't going to let the rest of us "walk" until Carol told them I was her cousin. Now I'm not really sure what they could have charged me with, but they did make mention of being an "accessory." An accessory to what, I'm unsure. Anyway, Carol tells them surely their kindness could extend to her cousin, right? Right.

She got me out of a bind that night, but more important we always had each other's backs. When her brother died, when my dog passed away, when I didn't get into Harvard, when she lost her first love to another, we were there for each other. I'll never forget how our fingers found each other, barely touching, looking at each other with "Oh Shit" written all over our faces. How just looking into her eyes calmed me down.

I'd spend countless nights talking till the wee hours of the morning with my best friend, Carol. I miss her, Blake. I don't even know her fate and all these images of her play in my head as if she's giving me one last view before her soul departs.

Huh, you and I, we never did discuss religion. Dare I ask?

Other than still going down to Willy's to dish out food, I spend my days with Mrs. Willard and Suzanne. It's the only thing I can think to do, but have to admit to being somewhat "zombie" like. It's enough for me to put one foot in front of the other. I'm just glad the art gallery has remained closed so I can spend my days in this manner…trying to locate Carol and trying to offer some help to the workers down at Ground Zero.

Maybe it's all that I'm dealing with, but I can't even go there with you on the demolition vs. collapsed building debate. I saw the footage of the planes hitting the building and that's enough for me.

Hopefully you've had some time to reconsider yours (and Robs) position.

I'm tired, so I'm going to end here.

Be well, be safe, Blake.

xo

Tara

"It is no good to try to stop knowledge
from going forward. Ignorance is
never better than knowledge"

— Enrico Fermi

———◆———

Tara My Love,

I'm so so sorry to hear that Carol has not turned up yet. I know that she is like family to you. I'm glad her mom has you to help see her through. I'm pulling for you both, trying to imagine how difficult this must be. How can this be happening?

I was able to reach Justin who'd just been released from the hospital. He has a broken leg, broken pelvis and was treated for a collapsed lung. He told me two custodians, guys I was friendly with, both were killed, and Tara, he confirmed that some guys were seriously injured in the subbasement from a large explosion. I know you don't want to hear it, but again I have to wonder why there was a large explosion in the subbasement when the plane hit eighty floors above. I didn't hear anything about it on the news, have you? What is going on?

I don't want you to think I'm crazy, but I can't help thinking now that there was another reason for those crates of explosives. For instance, did you know in a controlled demolition they always blow out the foundation first to weaken and aid in the collapse? Which lines up with the explosions Juan, George and Justin say happened in the subbasement.

Rob has some good yet disturbing points. I think I mentioned to you before, that Rob graduated from M.I.T. and was recruited by NASA. He opted to make his life here in Maine but NASA fought pretty hard to get him to reconsider. He was tops in his class, so I believe him when he tells me it is impossible for jet fuel to heat to the point whereby it could ever melt steel. Plus, according to the science book I read, steel melts at 2,800 degrees. Remember, jet fuel, which primarily is kerosene, burns at 575 degrees.

Rob believes explosives were purposefully used to bring the buildings down. That our original theory about insurance fraud is a much bigger act of treason and it appears the terrorists weren't the only ones involved. Wow, can't believe I wrote that line. Still, when I think about the crates of explosives, the response those guys had to seeing Joe and me, and witness two behemoth buildings built to withstand even the impact of a much larger plane, collapse into their own footprint. Then learning about pryoclastic clouds and how and when they appear? What am I suppose to think?

Things aren't adding up.

Or, maybe they are, but it's a scary alternative.

Did you know that no steel structure building has ever fallen from fire before? In fact, when I went to the library this morning I located an article about a company, British Steel Building Research group, who two years ago wanted to establish the strength of steel. They burned six buildings, and in each case the steel structure remained standing, even when the fire reached the burning point of steel. And believe me they weren't using jet fuel! It's right on-line. Go to British Steel Building Research group and tell me how it's possible the steel structures they used in their research remained intact.

Also online is an office building in Spain that burned in a raging inferno for twenty hours. TWENTY HOURS! The firemen had a hard time even getting close to it to put it out, yet after intensely burning twenty hours the steel structure remained intact. The Towers went down in less than 90 minutes and this from a poorly burning fire?!

There was an initial huge inferno upon the plane's impact, which was probably the lion's share of the fuel burning up. How could there still be enough fuel to run through the building and melt steel? Please don't think I've gone off the deep end. There is a lot of stuff to reconsider about what we're being told happened on Sept 11th. I have this insatiable appetite for any information regarding that day.

I have thought much more about those IRS agents who visited my mom and Mrs. Ward. I am certain they are affiliated with, if not the actual men, who chased me that night at the Towers. Because of what I saw and their inability to stop me, these men must be caught up in the 9/11 tragedy and won't stop until they find and then silence me. I believe I stumbled upon something that is bigger than insurance fraud. This is so big. This is a moment like the Kennedy assassination when they denied there was a shooter on the grassy knoll. Look what happened to Oswald! I'm terrified.

Your images of Carol, like a film reel, struck me. You always hear about a film clip of your life playing out at the moment of your death, but what if it's the reverse? What if the dying person sends images out to loved ones, and that's what you were receiving? I love the way your mind works, Tara.

OX,

Blake

P.S. To address your question about religion, I'd have to say I'm spiritual, not religious. I was raised Presbyterian. You were raised, Catholic, right?

"Refusal to believe until proof is given is a rational position; denial of all outside of our own limited experience is absurd"

— Annie Besant

Hey Blake,

Don't take this the wrong way, but what the hell are you talking about? The Towers were brought down by a controlled demolition? Come on! Who would do such a thing and more important, what possible reason would they have? And what about the planes flying into the buildings? You saw the footage on TV. How do you explain nineteen terrorists seeking revenge on the U.S.? How do you explain the planes? The crashes?

Come on, Blake. I know you're scared about those guys and I don't blame you, but you're spending way too much time listening to Rob, who sounds like a conspiracy theorist nut. He may be smart, but sometimes smart people don't exhibit common sense. Sorry, don't mean to be harsh about this, but your letter has me spinning.

Spend a day doling out food to the workers and tell me anyone but the terrorists had a hand in this. Please. It's not possible. And to Rob's opinion that the explosives you saw that night were all part of the "plan"? Well, the jet fuel may have ignited them, but certainly explosives weren't purposefully placed throughout the entire building. You saw them on one floor, right? It doesn't mean there were bombs planted in the subbasement, or that this was all part of a larger plot. Who could possibly benefit, other than the terrorists, from such destruction? I'm sure the explosives you saw is what we talked about and you originally surmised — insurance fraud. How else to explain its presence? I've been giving it more thought. You yourself said the building had a lot of leaseable space yet to fill. Causing damage on one empty floor makes sense if you're looking to pocket some needed cash, but to take out the whole building? Come on!

Besides, I heard an expert yesterday talk about the heat that was built up in the elevator shafts. That it caused them to explode, so when reporters, firemen and policemen talked about hearing explosions going off in the buildings, what they actually were hearing was the elevator shaft blowing apart, which weakened the structure. Imagine how much fuel was expelled after the planes hit!? They were gassed up for cross-country flights. Those terrorists knew what they were doing when they selected those flights.

You do realize that all it takes is one little spark for fumes to ignite, right? Fumes, yes fumes…not fire, not smoke, but the fumes from the jet fuel. Did Rob forget to account for the fumes?

What does Rob say about the nineteen terrorists? Were they handed a script and told to commandeer planes to crash into buildings? Oh, and by the way, make sure that you do so at this exact time so we can detonate some bombs and let the Twin Towers fall? How does he account for the terrorists?

I see what's on TV, I witness what is happening right outside my door and can't believe that you're sitting up in Maine harboring these thoughts. It's time to get back to the city. Time to get back to reality! Sorry Blake, but as I said, your letter has me in a tailspin wondering what is going on up there.

Yes, I admit to being scared for you. I don't know. I'm so confused by this whole thing. The world has turned upside down. I'm back to work on Monday and can't imagine getting excited over selling artwork. It seems as if a wall of tears is just waiting to be shed, but I can't cry yet. I have to stay strong for Carol's mom and for the volunteers who come into Willy's.

One of the volunteers came in this morning with tears streaming down his face. He's an insurance broker who took time off to help at Ground Zero. This morning he found a body. So sad. Everyone was telling him that the person's loved ones would be appreciative that he located their body, but there was no consoling him. I don't think he's going to come back. Witness a scene like this and tell me it wasn't pure evil that played a hand in the Towers coming down.

We're still searching for Carol, still wondering what happened to her and with each passing day the horrible truth becomes more apparent. Still I go over to Mrs. Willard's every day after serving breakfast at Willy's, and we make the same circuitous route we've taken since September 12th. Three hospitals, five makeshift triage centers, and countless locations where her picture is posted to make sure it's still there. Yesterday we saw that someone put a photograph of their loved one over Carol's and we were reluctant to remove it. Instead we found a corner of the board and put a new one of Carol up. How can we claim that one person's loved one is more important than another?

With your latest letter I must admit I'm concerned about you. Please stop looking for things that aren't there. As we talked about, come back to the city, come stay with me, and we'll both go to the officials to tell them what you saw that night. With any luck we'll get you some police protection.

xo

T

"Power is not a means, it is an end.
One does not establish a dictatorship
in order to safeguard a revolution;
one makes the revolution in order
to establish the dictatorship"

— Orville

—◆—

Tara,

My love, you say "don't take this the wrong way," but your anger at my doubts of what the TV is telling us is coming through loud and clear. I am not studying all this stuff because I want to be difficult or contrary to what seems obvious by what, and by how, we are being informed. I want to know the truth and I'm sure you do too.

I know you are right there dealing with all the heartbreak first hand. You haven't had time to stop and think about all the things I am learning. You didn't see the cases of explosives or get shot at for seeing what I wasn't supposed to see. Or having my where-abouts sought after by unexplainable men showing up at friends and families doors who know me. In fact, I talked to my mother again and guess who showed up for the second time? IRS agents! Not only is there no chance of my having any tax problems, but they showed up twice? They asked her if she had heard from me. Think about that, Tara. They go to Ohio twice to interview my mother?

I know about the planes hitting the buildings. I've seen the drumbeat videos shown over and over. You ask me about the nineteen terrorists seeking revenge on the U.S. Well I haven't seen one video or security tape of any terrorists boarding any air-planes. Have you? And revenge on the U.S. for what? Fifteen of the so-called terrorists were from Saudi Arabia. They are a very good ally of the U.S. Why would Saudis attack us?

Have you ever heard of the close family ties between the Saudi royal family and President Bush's family? Did you know that in the past thirty years Saudi Royals and their associates have given the Bush family and their friends $1.4 billion of business? Astounding!

Is it any wonder why the White House approved six private jets and nearly two dozen commercial planes to fly 142 Saudis (including twenty-four members of the Bin Laden family!) out safely at a time when no one else was allowed to travel? Doesn't it strike you as odd that not one of those 142 Saudis were interviewed — not even Bin Laden's family? And this after accusing the man of being the mastermind behind 9/11! Two days later we red carpet flights out for his family and others. Please!

Cheney and Condoleeza have been saying for a while now that they have all kinds of evidence on how this all points to Bin Laden. Since we're ready to go into Afghanistan, I think we're owed at least one bit of proof. Where's the proof?

I find it interesting that Bin Laden, a guy who admits to every evil hand he's had in things, says he had nothing to do with 9/11.

Do you think they'll ever share the proof or are we going to blindly go into war on Cheney and Rice's promise of proof?

And you have made my good and very intelligent friend Rob sound like some crazy, when he is looking for the truth. The way you call him a conspiracy theorist nut. They have made conspiracy a bad word. Just like Liberal. You are supposed to think exactly what they tell you on TV or you're somehow anti-American. It is good that Americans are pulling together at this very tough time, but I fear we're not pulling together against the right persons. We need to find out the truth. Please stop "spinning" about all this and get some traction on what we're discovering.

Doesn't it strike you as ironic knowing what I observed and the strange way the buildings came down so fast? In their own footprint! I know I keep banging this drum, but for the love of common sense, is anyone really buying these buildings collapsed?

I know the planes were loaded with fuel for transcontinental flight, but most of the fuel exploded in the air upon impact. We all saw the huge ball of fire when the second plane hit the building. AND, it's a scientific fact that jet fuel is mostly kerosene and could never be hot enough to melt steel, yet we're told this is exactly what happened. It's not scientifically possible!

We don't know who would benefit from such a specific destruction, or what is going to come down because of this. Time will tell.

Let me share the most frightening revelation. This whole event plays into Cheney's and Rumsfeld's view of the world. How? Cheney and Rumsfeld are members of Project for a New American Century. This is an organization with political ideologues. They wrote a detailed plan that includes invading Afghanistan, Iraq and the Middle East. Their goal? Make America the only super power in the world by gaining a foothold in the Middle East. They openly state that the transition would be a slow one absent a catalyzing and catastrophic event like a new Pearl Harbor! Their words, not mine. Both Cheney and Rumsfeld are proud members of this neocon group! We've already started a war in Afghanistan, what's next? A war with Iraq?

Would it surprise you to learn that Cheney ran several war games in the northeast portion of the U.S. on the morning of 9/11? These involved hijacking scenarios drills of major airlines and while many of these drills were planned for later in the year, Cheney insisted they all be run on that day. This was unheard of, in fact one official called it "unprecedented." In one case the emergency responders thought the distress call was coming from this simulated drill and didn't respond right away.

Did you hear Cheney had a "stand down" order for the two hours the attacks occurred? What was that all about? Why isn't anyone questioning him about not sending up Norad fighter jets when we were under attack? This along with the unprecedented hijacking scenarios Cheney ordered? Isn't this more than a little suspicious?

As for explosions occurring in the elevator shafts — I haven't heard about that. I heard that the sprinkler systems were working to help put out the fires because water came out of the elevators when they came to the lobby. Hard to imagine the heat became so intense as to explode the elevator shaft.

Yes, there may have been fumes that possibly even ignited, but this still wouldn't have melted steel. And these buildings had incredible steel core columns in the interior of each. If there was a pancake collapse like we have been told, those core columns should have been still standing. Rob and I went online and took a look at the architectural renderings of the buildings. I won't go into it here (these letters are getting quite long!) but encourage you to look at how they were constructed and tell me why the core columns aren't still standing.

I have talked to my friends who worked in the subbasement. I think they know where they were when they were injured. What reason would they have to say the explosions happened just before the planes hit? How do you think they feel knowing that and being told it's not true?

I have heard stories of people who came running from the buildings shouting that there were explosions going off all over the place. I saw many news reporters talking about the explosions and heard one fireman's account of the floors being blown up one by one just like it was some kind of demolition (his words, not mine!).

I know you are witnessing so much outside your door. My heart goes out to you for what you have to endure. I am so proud of you and what you are doing for our fellow New Yorkers. The whole world is shaken up by this, but no one feels it in their front yard like the people of the city.

I wish I could be right alongside you, helping. I want to know what happened to my good friend, Joe, visit Juan, Justin and George and hold you in my arms.

I don't imagine you are in any hurry to return to work but maybe it will be good for your tortured soul. Oh Tara, this is sure not what we envisioned for our future. I believe it was "pure evil" that brought about this horrible deed just like you do. It will be an event that is going to change life as we know it. It already has. My searching for a different possible truth than the one we are being told about is for truth itself, and our missing friends. I am not searching for things that aren't there. Please don't think that way. I am learning things that "Are." I'm fortunate to have the time to use the computer in the library. Other than a few children's story hours, hardly anyone uses the library so I'm free to spend time on one of the two computers there.

I know it doesn't make sense to you right now given the war-torn world you are witnessing and trying to help out. I can't stand the thought of creating any distance between us. I just feel like I want to know truth, "9/11 truth" has a meaningful ring about it. I want to do it for Joe, Carol, and what may be thousands of others who were taken from us by pure evil. I can't let this evil come between us my love. Please try to understand…I miss you so.

OX

Blake

"Dogmas — religious, political, scientific —
arise out of erroneous belief that thought
can encapsulate reality or truth. Dogmas
are collective conceptual prisons. And
the strange thing is that people love their
prison cells because they give them a sense
of security and a false sense of 'I know'"

— Eckhart Tolle

Wow Blake,

I've never seen you so riled up before. Granted, we've only known each other a short while, but I could practically hear you screaming at me throughout your letter. I didn't mean to upset you and certainly didn't mean to lash out at your friend, Rob, who I haven't even met yet. I have long thought that without conspiracy theories we would never get to the truth of matters, sometimes.

To me, questioning authority, questioning what we see is not only important, but needed.

It just feels as if there's a bit of paranoia coming from the north. Believe me, I get it! I understand why you of all people are looking for clues as to what transpired September 11th.

To your point that you hope I want to know the truth as much as you do, of course I do. I'm not a dullard, Blake, and I don't blindly accept everything the media purports, but find it hard to reconcile the images of those planes going into the buildings with an overall sinister plan to take down the Towers. How do you account for fifteen of the nineteen terrorists coming from Saudi Arabia? Why wouldn't they have come from Iraq or Afghanistan? Granted, we know the Taliban are in Afghanistan so that's where we have to take the fight, but why not have them all hail from those two countries? That is, if the neocon group and Cheney and Rumsfeld, as you are implying, are behind it.

What's most troubling is even after seeing all the footage you think there was someone other than the terrorists involved. I am decidedly in your corner when it comes to the explosives you saw, the unidentified men looking for you, and Joe's disappearance.

Get it, got it.

Instead of thinking the terrorists were part of this overall sinister plan, what would you say to this scenario? In an attempt to collect money for space not leased, explosives are brought in to damage one of the floors. I'll even go along with Rob's theory that this would have been blamed on terrorists. Explosives are placed, plans are made, and then by coincidence terrorists hijack planes and crash them into the buildings. It's an unfortunate set of circumstances, because the explosives are already in place. The fumes from the jet fuel ignite a fire and set off the explosives, further weakening the structure of the buildings. If not for the explosives perhaps the Towers would still be standing. Instead of "blowing" up one floor, the buildings came down.

While there is evidence humans have a tendency to blindly follow along, I'm not one of them. Guess I'm taking this a bit personally, eh? I too want to know the truth. I too want to understand what happened that day. My best friend, Carol, is gone, and in addition to others that I've told you about, I recently learned that Mrs. Casey down the hall lost her brother. Did I tell you, Ed, the short order cook at Willy's, lost a couple of friends and my landlord, Mr. Wilcott, his wife is among the missing. This is just a small sampling of people who have been affected by this tragedy.

I agree with you that the buildings came down very fast and in the spirit of showing you that I'm paying attention, I'll tell you that I checked and there was 92,000 tons of steel used in the construction of each building. That's an incredible amount of steel and I'll admit that from a common sense point of view, it's hard to imagine this amount of steel collapsed in just a little over an hour. And both buildings? That's pretty suspect too. So you see, I do pay attention and I am taking in everything that you're writing.

As for Justin and your other friends who were harmed by explosives that went off in the subbasement before the planes hit, all I was trying to point out is that with everything going on that day I wouldn't be surprised if Justin and others were disoriented. You have to allow for misremembering, right? I recently read where even eyewitness accounts of a crime are not always valid.

A poor woman who was raped, and left for dead, pointed to the defendant as being her rapist. After ten years in jail they found through new DNA technology that he wasn't the guy. She could have sworn it was him and actually got up on the stand and *did* swear it was him. I'm just a little suspect about eyewitness accounts from individuals who experience trauma, particularly during the unfolding event.

As to your comments about Cheney, all I can say is I never liked the man. As to your comments about Bush and the money his family has received from Saudi Royals, all I can ask is then why are most of the hijackers from Saudi? Yeah, I know I'm repeating myself, but still, why? If Bush were involved wouldn't he try and pin this on terrorists from another country? Yours and Rob's theory isn't holding up on this point.

Your letter doesn't mention when you're returning. I fear your timeline has been moved and honestly Blake, I will be beyond crushed if this is true. I want you to come back to the city to get this all straightened out. Homeland Security would be interested in your finding explosives in the Towers before 9/11.

And it might help them figure out how and why the Towers came down. I'm certain this type of information would not only be helpful, but they would be able to set you up in a witness protection program, particularly when they hear there are men looking for you. If you want, I can explore who you would talk to and how to keep you safe.

This event is big (understatement) and any help in sorting through what happened would be welcomed. I just don't want you to get lost in the process. I don't want you to wind up hiding out in Maine for the rest of your life. You had dreams of returning to the city, going back to school, and dare I say it, spending time with me.

What about Joe? What about Mrs. Grabowski?

Yes, I'm continuing to dish out scrambled eggs before I head off to work and no, it doesn't get any easier...my heart is heavy, my mind is reeling. I don't need to be scolded like a child for suggesting another alternative to all that you and Rob are discovering. You didn't come across THAT bad, but I guess I don't want any tension between us when the distance already creates enough of a wedge.

I'm holding you close Blake with wide opened arms. Awaiting your return, awaiting your next letter. And awaiting your next call (hint, hint). Please know I am paying attention and yes, even though I'm witnessing a war-torn scene outside my window every day, I often look up in the sky and welcome hope into my heart.

xo

Tara

"The more original a discovery, the more obvious it seems afterwards"

— Arthur Koestler

My Dear Tara,

I'm so sorry if I came off angry sounding. I don't think I've ever been angry with you yet. It's just the stuff I've been learning through Rob and my research down at the local library has made me angry. I imagine it is coming through without volume. I am glad to hear you are not so troubled by what we (mostly Rob) have been turning up. Questioning authority you say. Maybe that is what this is. Have we come to the point where the TV is authority? Does common sense no longer prevail?

Thank you for understanding that what is commonly considered conspiracy theories can sometimes better be described as the truth. Although you do leave it open that this sounds like paranoia from the North. I might better describe our findings as the cold wind of reality.

92,000 tons of steel. You think the Towers could be brought down with kerosene? Twice? This steel-melting story has got to be the biggest load of crap I have ever heard. This blew me away. Really. How much more proof do we need?

I have not heard any explanations as to why fifteen of the so-called terrorists were Saudis. I know that is where Bin Laden is from but I'm wondering about him as well. It seems like they were already accusing and convicting him of this atrocity within a few hours of the planes hitting. I know he has been responsible for some horrific terrorist attacks, but never in the U.S. It would be a major coup for him. Look, I don't know for sure who did it; I'm just not accepting the authorities' conclusions. Not yet. This reminds me of how fast they nailed Lee Harvey Oswald for the assassination of JFK. He was the sure guilty party, when we hadn't even scratched the surface of that mysterious crime.

Since our shared interest in 9/11, Rob has been coming to the cabin more than usual. We watched a TV report the other night on how airplane fuel weakened the steel trusses, but Rob pointed out that they didn't even mention the incredibly sturdy forty-seven core columns of structural steel that made up the center of each tower. Have you had a chance to look at the architectural drawings of the Towers? Did you see the huge forty-seven core columns? The special only commented about the steel perimeter, never once acknowledging the core column. They made it appear as if the floors were weakly hanging there, almost waiting to fall. I'm sure the average American just believed what they were seeing and I might have too. But Rob is no average American and he spoke right up about the columns absence. Then when we confirmed this stuff online — I wondered who put together this special, and where they were getting their information! Were they purposefully hiding something real important from us? Why??

And why didn't the special provide us with the burning property of jet fuel. Were they told not to include this information? Didn't anyone ask the question? Didn't any of the scientists they hire know jet fuel is mostly made up of kerosene and could never burn hot enough to melt steel? According to the research I did at the library:

> *"jet-aircraft engines use fuels which are less flammable, making the fuel easier to transport and handle"*

I see you've been thinking about our initial theory of insurance fraud. Well I'm sure insurance will be collected, for sure. How much, who knows? But this has the appearance of something much larger than that.

I'll say it again — THE BUILDINGS COLLAPSED IN THEIR OWN FOOTPRINT. Which means they were demolitioned. Which means someone placed explosives (yes, probably the ones I saw) in the sub-basement of the building. Which means someone was at the controls, because yeah, Tara, the only way to enact a demolition is to do so via electronics. I wonder where the base of operations was located? They had to be close enough so the chargers could be ignited, yet far enough away to avoid injury.

Granted, I really don't know much (and not sure I want to know any more) about demolition, but let's be honest, if anyone performed a simple research project at the library they'd see it doesn't take a brain to know what's going on here. The explosives had to have been tripped by an electronic device. Whose hand was on that device is anyone's guess. Are Rob and I the only ones questioning this stuff? I'm doing research online and finding all sorts of information.

I'm hesitant to talk to anyone up here since I'm keeping a low profile, but can't imagine we're the only two catching on.

I have one more burning issue that I really am intrigued by. I will know by your reaction if I am onto something. I find it incredibly unbelievable that no one is talking about the fact that my former security company was headed by President Bush's youngest brother Marvin. I never saw him there or knew of his direct involvement in any way, but still, how can a fact as significant as that go unreported?? You haven't heard anything about it have you?

Securacom, the name of my former company, has been mentioned several times in the news, but not one mention of its head person. The only thing I can think of is the media doesn't want any mention of him so as not to cause embarrassment for the President.

It is tragic how many people this affects even in just your building. I won't ask how Carol's mother is doing. I'm sure it is too sad for you to relay.

I know this goes without saying, but I want to remind you not to tell anyone of what I saw at the Towers that night. I want you to do your wonderful work and stay removed from anything about me. Remember there are some not too friendly men looking for me. I was heartened by your statement of looking up into the sky and welcoming hope into your heart. That is what you are to me Tara...hope in my heart.

OX

Blake

"That thorny path, those stormy skies,
  Have drawn our spirits nearer;
And rendered us, by sorrow's ties,
  Each to the other dearer"

— Bernard Barton

Ah Blake,

This morning was Carol's memorial service. Mrs. Willard arranged a beautiful ceremony incorporating some of Carol's favorite songs throughout the program. This was extra special because her mom is inclined to like religious songs, but understood this was a day to honor Carol. I reminded her it was also a day for her to seek solace, that if she felt more comfortable with the standard religious tunes Carol would understand. She said she didn't want anything more than her daughter to be able to look down from heaven and know that her mother not only loved her dearly, but knew her well enough to play some of her favorites. The one that got everyone going was a sweet Melissa Etheridge ballad that Carol always played to lift her spirits. Not everyone in the church knew this, but the mood shifted as words of hope were sung. I swear a ray of sunshine came though the stained glass window of the Virgin Mary right at that moment. At the end of the ceremony two bagpipers stood on either side of the church doors filling the air with the mournful call of that beautiful instrument.

I'm not sure why I'm fixated on the music. I guess because when we were teenagers it was a bone of contention between Carol and her mom. Maybe it's because it's the first time I heard contemporary music in a church. Maybe it's because I find so much joy (and sorrow) with music. I don't know.

Father Feeney said the mass, which was good. He's known Carol all her life so he was able to provide some personal anecdotes. Mrs. Willard asked me to speak. For the most part, all I could do was stand up at the pulpit and cry. I knew this is what I was going to do so I wrote a piece about having nothing to say for surely there are no words for such sorrow. I just wanted to stand there and cry and hope that through my tears, through the expression of my sorrow, everyone who loved Carol could see the depth of my loss and perhaps this would touch inside them a memory of Carol. That in our shared pain we would connect to her being, her presence. Words could never substitute. I said something along these lines. Forgive me for not remembering what exactly I said. Suffice it to say it was said through a torrent of tears that at times caught my breath, threatening to do just what I feared — stand there and cry. Sobbing, my body shaking, racked and rocked with sorrow, this day has been tough for me and I honestly am having trouble stringing words together in a coherent sentence.

After the service we went to Mrs. Willard's place and had a nice, subdued gathering. Suzanne, Michele and I played "hostesses," not wanting Carol's mom to lift a finger. Over 200 people streamed through her apartment. Thankfully, she has a pretty good size one for New York, but can you imagine? At the memorial service there must have been 500 people there! And Blake, you're not going to believe it, because it took a moment for me to believe it — Mayor Guiliani came to the memorial service and then to Mrs. Willard's apartment to express his condolences. She doesn't know him from Adam and with all the memorial services and funerals to go to he came to Carol's? Mrs. Willard was so touched and so was I. Carol, nor I, ever did really care for him. I have to think she's smiling at the irony of having never voted for the man, but he nonetheless came to express his condolences.

I reread your letter several times trying to get a feel for exactly where you sit with all of the 9/11 stuff and have to say that in some ways your recent letter scares me more than the one before. I prefer that you be angry about your situation then be diving deeper into the rabbit hole on the conspiracy stuff. As I said before, I agree with you that the Towers coming down in such a quick fashion is suspect. I'll even grant that jet fuel would not melt steel, yet would you agree that the fuel weakened or compromised the steel? Would you consider the fuel, once ignited, caused the crates of explosives you and Joe saw to detonate?

The reason the government focused on Bin Laden so quickly is because the main hijacker's luggage was mistakenly left in Portland, ME, and never did get on the connecting flight. In his luggage was information about Bin Laden, the other hijackers, and details about their plot. Now I have to admit when I heard this I was suspicious. Certainly the airlines don't always get luggage transferred to connecting flights, but this particular luggage didn't get through? And he just happened to lay everything out in a nice, neat fashion? Another point that has bothered me is that his Will was contained in his suitcase. Now why would someone who is planning on killing himself pack a Will in a suitcase destined for the same doomed flight? See? I'm starting to think like you and Rob.

Then I got the news about Carol and frankly put all these thoughts aside. I guess the image of the planes going into the buildings, the other two in Pennsylvania and the Pentagon, is enough information for me to conclude that terrorists were involved with all of this.

No, I never knew that Marvin Bush was the head of the security company for the Towers. Wow! You're right though. He wouldn't have any day-to-day overview of what goes on at each property, but still...it is pretty amazing. Learning this is like the day when the election between Gore and Bush was up in the air because of Florida where Bush's brother, Jeb, was the Governor. It was bizarre then, it's bizarre now.

I should write more, but honestly, I'm worn out from the day's events and need to get this into the mailbox. It pains me how long it is between letters for us. Our phone calls here and there sustain me, but I could surely benefit from your arms around me as I fall to sleep.

My sweet Blake, as always, I wish you were here.

xo

Tara

"A dictatorship would be a lot easier —
so long as I'm the dictator"

— George W. Bush

Tara, Tara, Tara,

My heart goes out to you, and Carol's mother. Your letter has brought me to tears. I'm thinking of you at her service in pain, and you trying to convey your lifelong feelings for her through your agony-wrought emotions. I'm sure it was impossible.

You, Suzanne and Michele were fantastic for Mrs. Willard. She probably feels like you were such a good friend to Carol and will undoubtedly transfer some of that love for her to you. I can think of no one more deserving. I'm trying to send some tenderness for one of the worst experiences of your life. Carol was the same as losing family for you. I'm so sorry for what you are going through, baby.

My problem is, it fuels my anger at the same time. I generally don't hold on to anger, I'm very quick to forgive. It's just that so much research is leading to a non-stop anger renewal. There are things that I'm finding out, Tara, that are keeping me from my usual forgiving mode. I don't want any of this to come between us. I see where it can be a problem. You are there going through all the day-to-day dealings of tragedy and loss, and you see me hidden away at the cabin unearthing all your world can't allow you to hear. And dare I say it, all our media, big business culture won't allow us to hear. Try to bear with me.

I appreciate your "getting" some of the stuff I have been trying to impart. The Towers falling like they did so quickly and the jet fuel causing a structural steel meltdown? I feel you're getting it, but then your depth of wanting to take in more becomes quickly shallow again.

I probably mentioned this before, but in case I haven't, Rob and I have been wondering where the Norad interceptor planes were on 9/11. Here you have four major airliners, presumably hijacked for an hour and not one Norad plane is dispatched? In case you don't know about Norad, whenever contact is lost with any airplane, fighter jets take to the air to investigate. This commonly occurs about 100 times per year and by 9/11 it had occurred sixty-seven times before. Always, ALWAYS, fighter jets responded within 20 minutes of the plane's signal being lost. On 9/11? With Cheney at the controls? Nearly two hours passed without any interceptor being dispatched. Mind you, most of the doomed planes were in the air for a good hour. There was even confirmation that a small plane was off course, in D.C. airspace. It was likely another hijack situation was in play, but no fighter jet was sent out to investigate! In fact, Cheney gave a "stand down" order! When told there was an unknown plane flying in D.C. and asked if Norad should be enacted, Cheney angrily stated, "stand down." He then told those in the situation room the order stands, effectively telling them to "shut up."

I have seen the flight school reports where the terrorists were supposedly training secretly so they could use that knowledge when they hijacked the airliners. These guys were just beginners at flying small planes like a Piper Cub. How am I expected to believe they killed flight attendants and pilots, then turned these giant jetliners around and flew a perfect course to New York City, Washington and Pennsylvania? Hitting the Towers and the Pentagon, perfectly.

Has anyone even wondered why Secret Service allowed Bush to remain in that Florida classroom after the 2nd plane hit? Surely, he would have been considered a target were we officially under terrorist attack and he remains sitting in a classroom *with children!* Reading a book? Why didn't the Secret Service squire him away to a safe location? Why did they risk the lives of all those in the school that day? His whereabouts weren't secret. How did they know a plane hadn't been hijacked and was headed to that school? What did they know that the rest of us didn't know? And why is it being reported that he witnessed the first plane ramming into the Tower when there's only one camera crew that captured the event and that tape JUST got released? How did Bush see the first plane ram into the Tower when, at the time, there was no footage?

Why did Rumsfeld tell Representative Christopher Cox before the 2nd plane hit that he's been around the block a few times and watch there will be another event? At that point everyone was speculating pilot error, why was Rumsfeld speculating an "event"?

I read in *U.S.A. Today* that an airport official was ordered to destroy all of his tapes of that day's activities. I mean does this sound like they are avoiding embarrassment, or covering up???

I saw a video of the crash scene at Shanksville, PA taken on Sept 11th, and there was no wreckage bigger than a telephone book. Just a big hole in the ground. Have you ever seen a crash site where there was no significant wreckage? Ever? Should I be suspending disbelief, or just stick my head in the sand completely?

I hadn't heard about the hijackers luggage being found at the Portland, ME airport. After reading what you wrote all I can say is, "Isn't that convenient?" Let me tell you about another very convenient thing. It was reported that one of the hijacker's passports was discovered on the sidewalk below what were the Towers. Not to be sarcastic, but HA! That means a paper passport fell from his pocket, coasted through a huge jet fueled fireball that was created when the plane exploded. This paper passport then floated down umpteenth numbers of floors, safely landing on the sidewalk already riddled with debris. Then, survived the Towers collapsing with 92,000 tons of steel along with pulverized ankle-deep powder, desks, chairs, bodies and still the "authorities" found it and get this…his picture was still intact! The corners on his passport were singed, but otherwise you can see, my believing public, this is the face of a terrorist! Oh, that jet fuel might have taken down tons of steel, but this paper passport miraculously survived! And look, this terrorist's name just happens to be on a sheet of paper in a conveniently forgotten piece of luggage at Portland Airport. Along with his name is the terrorists' dastardly blueprint for 9/11.

We vilify, quantify and are captivated by storylines that are fed to us every day. We're so busy trying to make a life for ourselves, trying to put our footprint on this earth we oftentimes don't pay close enough attention to what's happening outside our front door. We're tired and frustrated, we want love, we want our contribution to be meaningful in all aspects of our lives, but we're walking a treadmill, blindly being fed from the idiot box.

Look how George Bush's ratings were in the crapper before any of this happened. Did you know prior to 9/11 that in the short nine months he was in office he spent 42% of this time on vacation? What about the questionable results of the 2000 Presidential election, being decided by one conservative Supreme Court Justice instead of the voting public…to Brother Jeb being the Governor of Florida which decided that fiasco…to now Brother Marvin in charge of security for the World Trade Center. There are a lot of things I find questionable about our new President. How he came, and now stays, in power. I'm still waiting to hear any news of brother Marvin's connection to this tragedy.

None of us like Bush, including Rob, but even I found a new level of hate for the man, after Rob showed me an online article from a London newspaper. Bush is quoted as saying, "It was amazing I won. I was running against peace and prosperity and incumbency." That was in June of 2001 our President was saying this and look at how the world has changed. No longer do we have peace, and I guarantee you that the prosperity the last administration brought to our country will be spent and we'll be in debt within a year. I see the wide open gape of the war machine, and it's looking for greenery!

Guiliani's ratings were in the crapper, too! The man committed political suicide and couldn't catch a cab to take him a block, that's how much he was hated. Now look at him. The Mayor of the United States! What's next? Is he going to run for President? Give me a break. Yet, it's conceivable. A month ago it wouldn't have been, but now he's gained political capital.

It's the storyline. The crap we're fed. Let's not consider how 92,000 pounds of steel comes crashing down in what by all appearances looks like a demolition. Instead, let's believe nineteen terrorists flew planes into buildings, which dispensed fuel, which started fires, which compromised the steel. Come on! Science proves otherwise.

What's the end game? It's certainly not insurance fraud. We've been down that path and this is much bigger than that…no, this is something that has to do with pinning the blame on Muslims. Bad Muslims — terrorist Muslims — for what reason? Are we going to declare war? How is that possible? The terrorists don't even have a location. Who do we confer war onto? Oh that's right, we're in Afghanistan with 11,000 troops. There are more policemen in NY than there are troops in Afghanistan right now. No, I don't think Afghanistan is the end game.

Tara, I don't know what to think. There's a reason all this happened though and in time we're going to find out the reason why. Look at all Rob and I uncovered so far! Certainly others are questioning what we're being told. Granted, being one of their loose ends I'm anxious to expose the whole scheme so I can get back to the life I once had.

I've been hesitant about telling you this, but when I called Justin today to see how he was doing he told me the IRS guys came to see him. Seems they are still looking for me. I never told him I was in Maine, just on vacation, and that's all he was able to share with them. Not that he would have told them anything, but I'm thankful I'm keeping my whereabouts private. Now these men are questioning my friends? Jesus, Tara, this is much too serious to ignore and points to another reason why someone other than the terrorists had a hand in this tragedy. If nothing else, someone was complicit in letting them plot, plan and execute. That "someone" is someone who knows I saw those explosives before 9/11 and wants to make sure I don't share this with anyone else.

I hope you can understand why I can't return to the city, Tara. I so want to be at your side. I so want to hold you close again. It just doesn't seem possible. It is just not safe for you, or me to come back now. Please understand Tara.

OX

Blake

"Usually when people are sad, they
don't do anything. They just cry over
their condition. But when they get
angry, they bring about a change"

— Malcolm X

Blake,

I understand, I get it. It would be dangerous for you to come back to the city.

Yet, let's talk about getting you out of Maine soon and talking to authorities who would benefit from knowing what you know. Given Homeland Security is a new organization, there is no way they are involved in this so why not talk to them? I made the offer before, and will do so again. Let me make some inquiries as to who you should talk to and let's get the ball rolling on this. In addition, let's find a media outlet that will tell your story and put your face out there so these men will be disinclined to hurt you.

Staying in Maine is not an option. Sooner or later you're going to have to leave the cabin, and sooner or later you're going to have to figure out a way to get your life back. Certainly there are selfish motives on my part to get you back here. Yet, realistically don't you see that getting you out of this bind is the most important thing you can do right now?

What are you doing to ensure you're safe? Other than hiding out at the cabin, that is. Do you think the longer you stay away these men will forget about you? You have no option here. No hint of safety unless you take measured steps. Instead of researching the melting point of steel, how about figuring out what you're going to do?

I'm a little ticked off at your comment about me starting to "get it," but then the depth of my wanting to know more becomes quickly shallow. Wow, no one has ever called me shallow before and I resent the implication. In dealing with Carol's death and the horror and devastation in the city, you're right. Maybe it's difficult for me to wrap my mind around all the things you and Rob are uncovering. Yet, Blake? I'm not a shallow person. I'm a reasoned individual who wants a little more facts before forming an opinion.

I already told you that the Towers coming down in a little over an hour seems suspicious. I offered up another plausible scenario that didn't involve government officials and big business nefarious plots. You never even gave me the courtesy of considering my alternative scenario. Instead you jump on Bush and Giuliani, in what I'm reading as an attempt to link them to this "storyline" you and Rob have concocted. I find it infeasible that the President of the United States and Mayor of New York were in cahoots to bring the Towers down. Are you kidding me with this stuff? Did they meet over a hoagie and decide to kill 3,000+ Americans? For what purpose? You think they are setting up to go to war? Why? Why would we want to go to war with an Arab country? I'm assuming our target would be Saudi Arabia since this is where most of the hijackers hailed from. So, to your way of thinking, Bush is going to enact war on one of our allies? Saudi Arabia? To what end? Are we looking for their oil?

Why enact war on Afghanistan?

Look, you make some good arguments. The terrorist's passport, which survived a fireball free-fall. The way the Towers came down, and the explosions in the subbasement (yes, I'm going to accept the firsthand account of your friends). The convenient missing luggage, and yes, I'll even concede that jet fuel could not have weakened the building. Still, those explosives you saw could have been placed in the Towers for another reason and COULD have been ignited when the planes hit and COULD have weakened the structure. I admit this doesn't tie in with why there were explosives going off in the subbasement, but some of your arguments don't mesh either.

And for the sake of argument, would you please consider this from another angle?

I know from my friend, Jack, who's a pilot, that it's harder to work the controls of a small aircraft than a large one. If your argument is that the controls are simpler on a small aircraft, you're wrong. Depending upon the aircraft, it's typically more of a manual operation on small planes so the terrorists taking lessons on a Piper Cub doesn't automatically make them incapable of handling a larger plane. Besides, no one knows for sure that the terrorists took over control of the planes. For all we know they could have breeched the cabin, stuck the pointy end of a box cutter to the throat of the pilot and told him to turn the plane around.

What about the plane in Shanksville? You mention there is no debris larger than a phone book and leave it at that, as if I'm suppose to make some connection to the size of the debris to it being a conspiracy? Are you implying that a plane didn't go down in Shanksville? What are you saying here? The debris was small because the plane nosedived into the earth. Witnesses talk of the plane coming down and one after another said they saw a big red fiery ball explode upon impact. God Blake, how could you possibly think there was no plane in Shanksville? That is, if this is what you're saying. Your letter confuses me so maybe you can bring me into the "depth" of your thinking. You know, since I'm here in the shallow end of the pool.

Can you tell I'm slightly annoyed and yet...

As always...

XO

T

P.S. Thanksgiving is five days away and here you are still in Maine. You left FOUR MONTHS ago! FOUR MONTHS!

"CNN is one of the participants in the war. I have a fantasy where Ted Turner is elected president but refuses because he doesn't want to give up power"

— Arthur C. Clarke

———◆———

Tara, Sweet Tara…

Happy Thanksgiving, Tara! Rob and I had a nice feast here at the cabin. Not the typical fare for Thanksgiving dinner as we feasted on bass Rob caught this morning. I prepared a pie and all the other fixings. Did you go to your parent's house for the holiday?

Though the last few years a group of my friends got together for the holiday, and while I miss them, I have to admit to not missing the city. It was kind of nice to kick back here with Rob.

I love how you want me to come back to the city. I don't find anything selfish about it at all. Wouldn't it be just wonderful if we could get on with our lives the way we thought we would before the world fell down around us? I would love to find time to feel sorry for us, and the incredible detour our life together has taken. It's just with all the loss and heartbreak you and I have seen come to pass, we are the lucky ones — we are both still alive.

I was afraid that you would take my "shallow" comments the wrong way and sure enough. I never meant that you were a shallow person by any means. I just meant that your perspective in all of this, like the rest of the public, is shallow. We have been told exactly what to believe about what they say happened. I am quite sure we have been lied to from the start.

Did you know the Russians spent ten years fighting the terrorists in Afghanistan? They lost mainly because the United States helped arm the Afghan people, which included the current boogie-man of the hour, Bin Laden. Most Americans have no idea about that.

You asked if we wouldn't attack Saudi Arabia, since fifteen of the nineteen terrorists were Saudis. I just figure for sure there is something about oil in all of this. Could it be the Saudis and the U.S. are in on this together? Why not? It gives both of our countries domination in the Middle East. Watch the price of oil and listen to the flimsy excuses our oil companies and politicians throw out to the public when the price goes up. Americans always believe whatever they are told on the matter.

You say you want me to go to that new agency with my story of what I saw at the Towers. Homeland Security, what a nice wholesome name for what appears to me to be Big Brother run amok. They are having a field day with our rights and individual freedoms. It seems Americans are in a state of mind now where they are so frightened that they are willing to give up liberties for security. I think it was Benjamin Franklin who said if you are willing to give up your liberty for security, than you deserve neither. We are not the countrymen we once were and we are buying into whatever they come up with. As much as I would like to be able to trust someone with what I know, I just can't trust anyone from this government. It was only a matter of months back when we watched this current administration be "installed" by a Supreme Court decision, instead of the votes of the American people.

Bush and his administration talk about the terrorists not restricting our freedoms and then form Homeland Security, pass the Patriots Act, and what is the end result? Our own government is restricting our freedoms. Didn't it make you wonder how they were able to have a document like the Patriots Act ready to go in such a short period of time?

Did you hear Bush say the other day, "This crusade, this war on terrorism is going to take a while." Um…crusade, Mr. President? You see this as a crusade? As in holy war? Frightening!

I don't trust the media either. Every magazine, newspaper, television network, and any vehicle for information is all owned by five multi-billion dollar corporations. That is why I can't think of any outlet I would feel safe sharing my story.

I have been thinking about those nineteen terrorists. I really don't believe they could have flown those planes such a long way and hit with such precision. And the calls they allowed the passengers to make to loved ones on the planes? I was led to believe cell phones don't work in planes. I may be wrong but that's what I heard.

And in Shanksville, the size of the debris does make me question what really went down in Shanksville. Frankly, Rob brought this to my attention. He made me go online (again) to look at scenes of plane crashes. Particularly, those that nosedive crashed. Have you ever seen pictures of a plane crash where there was no wreckage? Look online and view photographs of airplanes that have taken nosedives. Rob had me look at them and still one can see it was a plane that crashed. No, Tara, there aren't small pieces of debris, but rather large chunks of the plane visible.

I have a lot to say about the Pentagon crash. Rob and I have found out things that surprise even us… BUT! I think I will save that for another letter before your head explodes and you tell the guys with the straight jackets where your crazy boyfriend is hiding.

I know you are still annoyed down at the shallow end of the pool (lol). If you dive a little deeper you will realize that things aren't adding up, and some form of reason must be applied to everything we're being told.

Mrs. Ward, my mother, Justin, and who knows how many more, have all been visited by "agents" from the IRS. Do you really think there is any safe place for me out there now?

I know you want me to return and I would love to. I hope you can understand how with these men looking for me, and my sincere belief 9/11 wasn't perpetrated by terrorists, alone, I hope you see why it's just too dangerous for me to consider returning right now. I know I can't stay here at the cabin forever, but I can think of worse places to hide out.

Rob has been great. He knows how I am missing you and always asks about you. Even though he knows how you feel about what we are unearthing. He has the greatest respect for what you are doing to help and heal those in Manhattan.

I think about what Rob could have been in the private sector. He was offered a teaching position at Columbia, which he turned down, and that NASA offer too. He was able to let go of the high paying, highly respected jobs, to live the life he knew was right for him. I admire his independence and willingness to live with less, so as to be able to enjoy the life he feels offers him so much more.

We have the best time when we go fishing. It actually gives us a break from all we have been learning and discussing. I caught a nice perch the other night. I don't think anything tastes better than fresh water perch. They really put up a good fight before you haul them in. We cook them over wood coals and feel like kings when we sit down to eat. Tara, you should taste what the rustic royalty dine on out here. I was wondering if you ever thought about living out in the country and away from the madness of the metropolis? I know that would be impossible now, with the Art Gallery and the heavy air of tragedy all about you. But maybe someday, when we are in some kind of normalcy, you might consider it? I write that word "normalcy" and yearn for it to be right around the bend. In the back of my mind I worry about when my life will ever be normal again.

I miss you everyday, Tara, and dream of our being together again.

OX

Blake

"We have met the enemy and he is us"

— Walt Kelly

Blake,

What can I say which hasn't already been said? You seem determined to not want to entertain any other plausible explanation than the one you and Rob have concocted. You seem destined to be in that cabin till the end of time. Can this Jersey gal see a life in the woods of Maine? Possibly. It'd be a far cry from what I'm used to, but I've always enjoyed being outdoors and I'm a big camper, which I can't say for most of my friends.

That's not the point though. Don't get me thinking of the possibility of spending my life in the woods, hunkered down, fearful of every knock on the door when it's time to step-up, Blake. If you had gone to the police prior to leaving for Maine, the authorities would have gone into the Towers and found the explosives. This could have prevented some of the devastation of 9/11. I'm not blaming you for this.... it's like blaming the victim for the crime. I'm just saying that the authorities would benefit from all that you know/saw and you can get back to living the life you envisioned. Yes, I KNOW you tried to get a hold of them, but what I'm saying here is maybe you should have run to the police station instead of running to the bus station.

I'm not in the best of moods, obviously.

How about college? How about finding a new job? How about Rutherford and your friends and your life?!

Ah, Blake, you say its fishy how cell phones don't work in planes, and question how on that one day a host of calls were made to loved ones. Well Blake, your research is a bit flawed. The passengers used the phones available on the planes, not their cell phones.

You wonder about Bush and the Saudi family's connection, yet don't make the connection that IF Bush had something to do with any of this, why would he implicate the Saudis? If the government had something to do with it, why have fifteen of the nineteen terrorists come from Saudi? You act as if the terrorists don't exist, yet I'm sitting here in Manhattan, a spectator to all they wrought. View the empty hole in the skyline where those two majestic buildings used to stand and tell me the terrorists don't exist. Attend the funerals, watch the countless parade of hearses going down the street every single day and tell me they didn't commandeer planes. You didn't even make note of my pilot friend's comment that it's harder to fly a small plane than a large one. It's almost as if you're taking all this information and fitting it in a predetermined theory that you and Rob have come up with on what happened that day.

Understandably, you are frightened what with all that has happened to you. And yes, maybe they do in some odd way have a connection with everything that transpired on 9/11, but maybe…just maybe… they don't. Maybe, just maybe, there is another logical reason. You're not going to know until you step away from the cabin, come back to NY and find someone you can trust who you can talk to. It's time to start getting back to living your life, Blake.

It's time.

Tara

P.S. It's also time to call me — it's been way too long!

"Beware of the man who works hard
to learn something, learns it, and finds
himself no wiser than before…he is full
of murderous resentment of people
who are ignorant without having come
by their ignorance the hard way"

— Kurt Vonnegut

———◆———

Tara, My Dear,

Yes, it would be good to talk to you now. We must soon. I can't believe all this stuff is taking us further away from each other than our geographical location has already. How could we not be speaking civilly to each other? I guess our different perspectives on this sad time in America has taken its toll. Almost like North and South when the country was really divided. North being Maine, and the South, New York City. I guess you are right, I have been writing more and calling less. I would say that may be because it is a little touchy now with our different takes on what caused this American tragedy. Perhaps it is easier to say the hard stuff with a pen than it is over the phone.

The IRS visited my mom again. I can't believe they aren't giving up and still calling on my mom? She's frightened for me, thinking I have tax problems and offered me money. She even offered money to the "agents," but they declined her offer (what does THAT tell you?). Assuming they could be tapping her phones I ended the conversation quickly, as I have with all my conversations with her. I'm sure she's thinking there is something terribly wrong. IRS Agents coming to see her and given she and I could stay on the phone for hours, and now I'm hanging up after two minutes? She knows something is up and is terribly frightened for me. I've enclosed a letter to her and hope you won't mind putting it in the mail for me. It would be best to put it in another envelope with a non-descript return address. Perhaps when you visit your folks in N.J., you can drop it in the mail there? I don't spell everything out to her, but want her to know I won't be in touch with her any time soon. I can't risk being found here, and fear sending her this letter with a postmark from Maine will expose me. How sad to think I won't be able to reach out to her any time soon. I just hope this letter explains enough about my situation to her and why she won't be hearing from me.

My Love, you are still the greatest comfort I have. And I remember that night when we talked till we couldn't talk anymore...the communication was in peak form and makes it hard to believe that we could come to this impasse. I'm sorry I told you to get some traction, and that my words made you feel like I was thinking of you as shallow. No matter what you do to derail all I have learned, I will never think of you as shallow. It's just that there is another truth from the one that your TV is telling you and I cannot betray that truth. Don't think less of me for that, as I think no less of you for all that you are learning or being "led to believe." Being misled is not your fault, when the whole country is being fed misinformation.

When I speak of Bush's connection to this, make no mistake I am not giving him any credit for the wicked wisdom of the whole attack. I don't think he could plan a simple White House evacuation, let alone a sinister "false flag" operation of this magnitude. It is just that they (being war machine, big business and zealots) needed a "war-minded" administration in place to make that happen. Thus, the insanity of the 2000 election scandal.

Do you remember how during that campaign they caught George W's camp using actual hidden SUBLIMINAL messages in his ads? How do we know they are not using this mind control in their reporting of what happened on 9/11?

I really don't believe we would have been "attacked" if they let the guy with over a million more votes cast (Gore) assume his presidency. Nine short months later we have this horrible occurrence. I really believe there is a connection — one insanity leading to another — and it has to do with power, the almighty dollar and greed. Let me please be wrong about us going to war or the price of oil going up dramatically. But there seems to be no mistake about the former. We're already in the caves of Afghanistan hunting down Bin Laden. I would venture a bet that we never find him! Scratch that, we won't find him with this administration — that I'm sure of! Better to keep the enemy out there lurking to instill fear.

As for 3,000+ people losing their lives to put money in someone's pocket, that is exactly what I am saying. If that is the price to go to war, than so be it. I'm sure the government will find fitting ways to honor those who gave their lives that day.

Let's face it, war is sure "good bu$iness" for some — military industrialist$ — contractor$ — politician$ propping themselves up on fear and phony patriotism. See if it all doesn't happen again Tara. Why can't anyone see?

You're probably thinking I've gone off the deep end now that I've flat out said our government and big business were in bed on this whole thing, but look at the evidence.

Did you know that on the day before 9/11, Rumsfeld made a public announcement that $2.4 TRILLION went missing from the Pentagon? $2.4 TRILLION? Are you kidding me? I never knew this, but Rob told me about it. I looked it up online (not that I doubted him) and sure enough $2 trillion is missing. Really? TRILLION? What a coincidence that this monster story is reported the night before 9/11. Knowing that the next morning it would be knocked off the radar screen by the biggest catastrophe ever to hit our shores.

It required a coordinated effort on 9/11 and no one is going to convince me it was nineteen terrorists alone who perpetrated this catastrophe.

We both agree that there is no way jet fuel melted 92,000 TONS of STEEL in a little over an hour. Heck, there's no way it would have melted steel if it burned for 1,000 hours!

My friend's firsthand accounts of explosions in the subbasement dovetails with the evidence that this was a controlled demolition. And look at the way the buildings fell in their own footprints!? CONTROLLED DEMOLITION!

Pyroclastic clouds, which only occur during demolitions or volcanic eruptions, rolling down the streets of NY as the Towers came down.

I'm not sure if I mentioned this before, but Rob and I heard a recording of a fire chief who had made it to the floor where one of the planes crashed. He tells his commander after being asked if he wanted additional help, "We have a few small fires and if we can get a couple of lines up here, I think we can get it under control." Or, words to that effect, and then the Towers collapse less than ten minutes later? Come on — this is a seasoned fireman! Don't you think he would have felt the "burning" steel? Wouldn't there have been more fires? Bigger fires? Particularly on the floor where the plane crashed? Come on!

Did you know that just a few days before, Raytheon had unusual stock options whereby they bet "ON" the company, while United Airlines and American Airlines, in an unusual stock agreement bet "AGAINST" their companies? I don't profess to know anything about stocks but find it highly suspect that a defense contractor, in an unusual move, bet ON itself and two airlines, in another unusual trade, bet AGAINST themselves. It's not me unearthing these truths — its stock analysts making these claims. And all three companies conducted unusual stock options days before 9/11? All three companies bet correctly? As I said, I don't understand it, but here's a piece I copied from *The Journal of Business*, which I have to assume, knows a thing or two about these things:

"A measure of abnormal long put volume was also examined and seen to be at abnormally high levels in the days leading up to the attacks. Consequently, the paper concludes that there is evidence of unusual option market activity in the days leading up to September 11 that is consistent with investors trading on advance knowledge of the attacks."

Rob told me last night that the Securities and Exchange Commissions (SEC), in a very rare move, deputized top officials from all three companies. I didn't know what he meant, but come to find out, if the SEC deputizes you, you are not free to talk about anything pertaining to the stock option. So let me get this straight. If you work at one of these companies and know of unusual activity or suspect something, if you're one of the thousands deputized by the SEC in the past 24 hours, you cannot talk about the options or else they'll haul you off to jail on a federal offense? Mouths are being closed, threats are being enacted and don't get me started on the Patriot Act and all that is allowing our government to do!

Shall I continue?

Let's not forget the explosives Joe and I saw that night. I no longer believe it was insurance fraud.

The "stand down" order by Cheney when an unidentified plane was circling D.C. The fact that not one fighter jet (Norad plane) was sent in the two-hour period we were under attack. When sixty-seven times in the past year they were dispatched within twenty minutes!

How could the Secret Service allow Bush to remain in that Florida classroom when the country was under attack? Bush issuing a statement that when he saw the first plane hit the Towers his first thoughts were "there's a pilot that doesn't know how to fly." What a flippant moronic comment which is revealing in that the footage of the first plane hitting the Towers came two weeks AFTER 9/11 whereas this statement from Bush was made the day of the attacks.

My personal favorite is the terrorist's passport. There is no rational-thinking person on earth who could fathom how a paper passport fell from a terrorist's pocket, floated through a raging fireball and landed safely on the sidewalk before the buildings collapsed. How fortunate to find it sitting on the sidewalk.

How about the three to six foot long steel columns embedded in surrounding buildings? These columns came from the Towers. Imagine the force of the blast that had to occur to hurl these columns horizontally into the façade of surrounding buildings! Unfathomable how no one questions how the appearance of porcupine-like steel is jutting out of the side of buildings when we saw the Towers collapse. Barring everything else that we know, doesn't this point to an explosion?

There is so much more, but you can see I'm building quite an argument to the media's take on all this…and let's talk about the media for a moment. What the heck is going on with them? Where are the investigative reporters? What happened to the footage of the reporters screaming there were explosions all throughout the buildings before the Towers came down?

Please let me know of any "independent media" you find that I would feel safe confiding my story in.

I have seen no one reporting anything to the contrary of the official story. From any outlet. As far as America knows there can be no other truth and we are not even being given the opportunity to question that "questionable theory" in any way. shape or form. Wrong or right, it's a one-way street, and thinking such as mine and Rob's will surely be looked upon as unpatriotic. How dare I let little glaring facts that don't add up to their truth get in the way of this out-of-control war machine! You can try and disprove my theory all you want Tara, and I hope you succeed. I'm sure not happy about my truth. Any more than I am happy about the one I have had shoved down my throat. I know better than some of the concocted malarkey they've had the courage to sell us. Come on!

Not only does our government enact the Patriot Act, they have used this situation to pretty much do whatever they please. Domestically and internationally. Secret wiretaps are now O.K. God knows what other assaults on our liberties are yet to come, and to what end? They can pretty much do whatever they damn well please now. It is not what our forefathers had in mind for the land of the free.

I have learned some very intriguing things about the Pentagon and its supposed attack. Have you ever wondered why you have never seen any video footage of the plane hitting the most secure building in the world? We've been shown the Twin Towers videos a thousand times and not one of the Pentagon. Do you know that within five minutes of the attack on the Pentagon the FBI went to surrounding buildings/businesses and confiscated their surveillance camera footage? Why can't they show us? How come they were able to dispatch agents within five minutes to grab surveillance footage, but couldn't mobilize Norad in two hours?

Here is the kicker, my dear. There are two split-second video shots of the Pentagon that got released. Neither show visible signs of an aircraft. And the hole from the supposed airplane is not nearly large enough for the hundred and fifty foot wingspan of the aircraft. Soon after the impact there was another explosion above the hole that changed the whole look of the crash scene. They kindly showed both images, but never did explain why the first hole, the one from the impact, wasn't large enough and never did explain what caused the second explosion. Hmmmm, more explosions. Does that sound familiar? Most of the fuel was ignited upon impact...sound familiar? No wreckage of that plane either...huh.

Oh, and that second hole? Still not large enough!

Imagine this...I saw a picture that was taken from the outside looking into the Pentagon. There's a paper book sitting on a little wooden table, both the table and the book are in perfect condition, right next to the crash entry. Wouldn't you think the fiery fuel would have at the very least caused small fires as what supposedly happened in the Towers? How is it at the point of impact a little wooden table and book remain intact?

And think about the approach of the plane diving from a high altitude to ground level to hit the Pentagon perfectly. The pilot initiated a perfect 180 degree turn, took out five (only FIVE!) lampposts and crashed into the side of the Pentagon which had just undergone construction to shore up the walls. Huh? Do you think that a pilot who had just learned to fly a Piper Cub could pull off an approach like that? It's nearly, if not completely, impossible. You know what else was amazing about this pilot's skills? He flew right into the bottom floor of the Pentagon and lo and behold was so technical in his approach, he never left a scorch mark, burn mark or bent a blade of grass on the entire lawn area. That's right. Even seasoned pilots marveled at this feat! Look at the photos and you won't see any, nada, nanno evidence that the plane ever touched ground.

I can't change reality to accommodate their "fantasy" even if America is doing just that.

I wish I could tell you I'm up here smoking some powerful pot to explain all this stuff, but it's not the case. The TV is getting all our countrymen stoned on the most unbelievable fantasy. It is very sad for me to watch. But I still love you, Tara. In all your angst and anger, please don't lose sight of that.

OX

Blake

"All changes, even the most longed for, have
their melancholy; for what we leave behind
us is a part of ourselves; we must die to
one life before we can enter another"

— Anatole France

My dear, Blake,

You start with Tara, my dear, and then launch into quite a scenario of all you have uncovered. Isn't it amazing how two guys with little to do, a library computer and fear in their hearts can come up with so much. Look at how duped all the rest of us are! Why we're so lucky to have you two brainiacs up there in Maine figuring this all out!

You ask where the investigative reporters are yet never account for the seasoned professionals who are being interviewed and questioned as to what transpired that day. Engineers, physicists, architects, terrorist specialists, all examining the information and giving their opinion, but none of what they uncover or surmise happened seems to matter to you or Rob. For instance, one engineer explained the explosions heard before the Towers came down — it was the elevators — the heat became so intense in the elevator shaft it exploded — yet every time I bring this point up you dismiss it. Before I get really going on this subject, let me just say that I agree with you. The theory about 92,000 tons of steel melting doesn't make sense. I have looked at the center steel core in the Towers and find it hard to believe it was compromised in the way they are explaining. It's hard to fathom how these columns came down with the rest of the building. REALLY hard to fathom!

Yes, I think the elevators exploded and yes, I think this weakened the structure, but agree with you that the central core still would have remained standing. I have no logical explanation for why the core isn't still standing. I'm anxious to have the architectural blueprints of the buildings put up on a screen and have someone explain how even the elevator shafts exploding could have weakened that core.

The terrorist's passport floating through the fireball and landing safely on the sidewalk to be found is odd. I'll even give you the missing luggage with all the documentation on what was going to transpire (including the names of all the terrorists) is suspect. It's not that I don't see that some of these things aren't adding up, Blake, it's just that your inability to consider another scenario is annoying and stubbornly blind. Your contention that our government and big business had something to do with all of this is frightening. Are you serious?

If I read your letter correctly you're indicating the government and big business were in on this from the get-go for the oil. So let me get this straight. "They" devise this plan to take down the Towers, kill 3,000 people and cause damage at the Pentagon so what...we can go after oil? Whose oil?

I'm assuming the only means to do this would be to go to war, right?

We're in Afghanistan now — is it an immensely rich, oil-producing country? Why would the government pin this on Saudi nationals? Granted, we're not occupying/going to war with Saudi Arabia but instead turned our attention to Afghanistan in an attempt to find Bin Laden. If Bush and the Royal Family are such good buddies, why would he cast a shadow on their country? Aren't our countries friendly with each other? If Saudi Arabia is in on all this, why wouldn't our government pin this on a huge oil producer who is also an enemy of the U.S.? Why not Iraq? We don't like Hussein, particularly after he tried to kill Bush Sr., so why not place the terrorists in Iraq? Why not enact war on Iraq? Why go to Afghanistan?

I can't even wrap my head around your theories so forgive me.

As far as Cheney giving "stand down" orders for the fighter jets? Where did you hear this? I haven't heard word one on this, and don't think this means I don't believe you. I just want to know where you heard it.

The Secret Service were probably fully aware of the threat to the President and would have taken him from that classroom if they had an inkling an attack was imminent in Florida. The northeast was being attacked, not the southeast.

Bush probably misspoke when he said he saw the first plane hit. You know how he's always trying to come across as that down-home kind of guy. Look how far he took it by buying that ranch in Crawford, TX, right before the election! And then he develops that slight drawl? That guy never had a drawl before he ran for President! I think he was just trying to allay people's fears, bring the tone down a bit and played with a scenario which wasn't true, but would make him look endearing. I too don't like the man and can't believe at this crossroads in our nation's history that he's (choke) leading us. Yes, some of the things he does seem very transparent to me — like the "hee-hee-hee, at first I thought the guy was a poorly trained pilot," or whatever it is he said, but some people eat this stuff up!

Look how many people bought all that Reagan sold and still to this day they invoke his name with such reverence!

Confiscating footage from the cameras surrounding the Pentagon doesn't surprise me. As far as the hole not being large enough for a plane to have made? I'll have to take a look at the photos you speak of and get back to you on that one. If it wasn't a plane, what are you "supposing" hit the Pentagon? I will admit that not having any burn marks on the grass is pretty unusual. Is that just a freakish thing? Could be.

Again, I'll grant you that there are some things that aren't adding up. It just doesn't mean that they add up in the columns where you and Rob are doing your additions.

The Patriot Act worries me as well. I can see where authorities need access to information, but this is giving them carte blanche and I'm not a big fan. It also surprises me how quickly the Patriot Act was enacted. It was almost as if it was sitting there waiting for the right moment to be shoved down our throats. I am NOT suggesting that the government had anything to do with 9/11 and this was one of the caveats. Not by any stretch. I don't think the government had anything to do with 9/11. How can I make the connection that our government had their fingerprints on the blueprint? Perhaps this is because I don't want to believe it. Besides, the terrorists have been angling for some time to take America down.

Hey, I have an idea, Blake. Why don't you and Rob argue for the other side? Why don't you prove the theory that it was the terrorists alone who caused this tragedy? Start from there and see how far you get. Sometimes arguing for the "other" side helps us to see a little more clearly.

I started this letter angry with you only to find that now I'm just tired. Tired of everything. It's hard to watch the news, hard to watch all the specials, and I'm scared, Blake. Scared that you and Rob are diving further down the rabbit hole. Does the name Ted Kaczynski mean anything to you? Secluded away in a remote place, far away from civilization, his mind snapped. Not that you're anywhere near where he is Blake, but I see the path and it's not a pleasant one.

I will say it one last time. Come back to the city, tell the authorities what you saw, and get your life back Blake.

It's here waiting for you, as is Rutherford.

Tara

"You can make people do
anything if they're afraid"

— Congressman Jim McDermott

My Tara,

I'm sure the last thing you want to hear is what new revelation I'm going to lay in your lap about 9/11. BUT!!! I am so wound up about this that I am sure I can bring you into the fold. Before you can say, "God give me strength." Please! Listen to what I have learned. You are right there in the city and I want to know if you have heard of Building 7. This was the third skyscraper that fell on 9/11 inside the World Trade Center complex. Did you even know a third building fell that same day? Most people have NEVER even heard of it. I tell you it is the "smoking gun"!!!

Building 7 was a forty-seven-story fabulous building. If it wasn't standing next to the Twin Towers it would be a most-impressive building. It truly was, and I remember it well. I had a certain pride in seeing to its security whenever I would enter it. This building was a structural marvel and contained a wealth of government offices and agencies. Inside you would find Secret Service offices, the Department of Defense, offices for the FBI and the CIA, the Internal Revenue Service, and the Securities and Exchange Commission. And most notable, Mayor Giuliani's Emergency Headquarters. The Securities and Exchange Commission held secret and confidential files on the investigations into WorldCom and Enron. The two shady financial giants with very friendly ties to our President George W. Bush. I'm sure you have heard about them in the news and their corrupt practices.

What is absolutely amazing about Building 7 is how and when it fell down, at 5:30 P.M. on September 11th. It fell for no apparent reason! It had three small fires in it and was hit by no airplane. Yet it fell at "free-fall speed" in what was an obvious demolition. I just learned about this myself. Seeing Building 7 come down, there is no question it was brought down by explosives. I bet 95% of Americans know nothing about it or that it even fell down. If this doesn't scream media cover-up I don't know what does. It was reported that it had fallen fifteen minutes before it actually did, on BBC TV. What does that say about knowing things in advance of them actually happening?? There were other buildings around 7 that were nearly destroyed from the falling debris of the Towers, yet their structures remained standing. Building 3's roof was nearly cut in half from the debris, but it didn't fall. Rob and I watched footage of Building 5 with flames leaping out on literally every floor, yet it didn't fall. I heard the Fire Chief say there were only three small fires in Building 7 and I believed him. There is no reason for him to lie. He was telling reporters that most of his men were battling the flames in Buildings 5 and 3. Those two were closer to the Twin Towers.

The fires at the Marriott they had gotten under control. He said pointing back to Building 7 that it was nothing to worry about. That was about an hour before Building 7 came down into its own footprint, at free-fall speed!

Were there things in there that needed to be destroyed before anyone could see them? I'm not just talking about the Enron and World Com files. Rob has always maintained that a demolition had to have a base of operations to bring the Towers down. There had to be someone far enough away to be safe, but visibly able to oversee the destruction and demolition. What better place than the security of Building 7? With the Mayor out wandering the streets, why didn't he use his Emergency Bunker? Why wouldn't he be in there of all days? Is it possible this is where the base of operations was located? The strange collapse, the fact that nearly no one even knows about this building falling. Why wasn't there more reporting on this massive building coming down? I guess you can see where I am taking this, Tara. It was like the "one" no one talked about. We saw the Twin Towers come down a thousand times on our TVs. But no one even knows about this massive structure, with all its significance entombed.

Guess what else was present in its destruction? Those pyroclastic clouds of dust. Why would collapsing buildings turn completely to dust? Why not chunks of misshapen concrete? How can Americans not question what they are being told? I should say what they are being "sold" from their little control boxes.

Where are the investigative reporters these days? Swept up in the tragic blindness of Patriotic fervor I suppose. I do my best to contain my inner fury as these things become obvious. I realize why "conspiracy theorist" has been turned into a dirty word. "Just believe whatever we tell you 'little Americans' and we will keep you safe." I shudder to think what else is coming down the pike.

You might be thinking I am losing my mind up here. While you have been sitting in the middle of catastrophe and dealing directly with the heartbreak around you. Just remember this is extremely painful and lonely for me, with each shocking revelation we uncover. I have to believe other people KNOW. I need to believe that!

How sweet it would be to find myself there at your side. Knowing what I believe and helping you deal with all that you're going through. I think about coming back to the city and then remember those men are looking for me. I think about what you suggest, telling someone about what Joe and I saw that evening, but who is going to believe me at this point? If I told the authorities about the explosives they would think me crazy and I would be dismissed...or

I'm afraid, even worse. Not to belabor the Kennedy Assassination, but many of the witnesses who saw it differently than what the Warren Report said happened; they wound up dead in a few years after that day. Many from strange circumstances. None of this stuff ever makes the news, and the official report is STILL, he was killed by Oswald. Even though a huge majority doesn't believe this it is still the "official" line. I feel like I have nowhere to turn but to you…and Rob.

I've long since given up on trying to reach Joe. Still wonder what happened to him, but I think I already know the answer.

I miss you my love.

OX,

Blake

"Talkin', talkin', talkin', talk
Baby let's just knock it off
They don't know what we've been through
They don't know 'bout me and you"

— Kanye West

Seriously Blake, seriously?

At first I thought building what? What building, and then got online and looked up Building 7. Okay, so it went down, which leads me to ask "so what?" There were multiple fires that compromised the building (please don't write back "see Tara, just like the Towers" and try and make this all connected). What's the big deal? Your point about all the government agencies being housed there and paperwork for Worldcom and Enron being destroyed is just a coincidence. There are coincidences, Blake. I mean, really? You're taking this conspiracy theory too far.

Blake.

Blake...

BLAKE! STOP!

You simply have to stop. Every building in and around the Towers had damage. Did you look into Building 3? 5? The Marriott? Geez, Blake. The fact that a building came down on the same day as the Towers fell should not be a surprise.

You seem to want to make the connection between Giuliani and his emergency headquarters being housed in Building 7 as proof this building was used for what? Demolition experts used Building 7 to set-up their control station? Before you danced around about Giuliani being part of this catastrophe and here you pretty much spell out that he was privy to everything going on. How could you? Giuliani probably saved more lives that day given his hands-on involvement from the moment the first plane hit. Have you seen him on the news? He's a broken man, Blake. Sad about what has happened in his city under his watch and has even showed up at all the firemen and policemen's funerals. He was at Carol's funeral! You honestly think someone could be aware of the impending death of so many and then bemoan the dead and injured? There is NO WAY Giuliani had anything to do with any of this and I'll say that Bush didn't either. Where the hell do you come off?

I find it odd that you believe the media issued a blackout re talking about Building 7, yet you apparently saw footage of its collapse. You can't have it both ways, Blake. Rationally one can see how the news of an unoccupied building that collapsed that day didn't warrant as much attention as what was happening at the Towers or in Pennsylvania or at the Pentagon. Building 7 coming down later in the day was a footnote to the greatest tragedy this country has ever witnessed or endured.

You keep bringing up the Kennedy Assassination as if this will explain everything that happened on 9/11. Yes, I agree that most Americans feel there was someone other than Oswald involved, but you can't arbitrarily make this statement and conclude that because of this event it follows 9/11 was an inside job. Most Americans, though agreeable to the prospect that someone else was involved in killing Kennedy, don't think it was the government. Scratch that. They don't think it was our OWN government. So could you also stop about the Kennedy Assassination connection? There is no connection.

Another irritant for me is your assumption that no one knows about Building 7. Have you and Rob canvassed the neighboring cabins? Have you gone into town? Taken a poll at the local library? From all accounts you are sitting there with only Rob as company. How do you know most people don't know about Building 7? I didn't know, but that doesn't mean others don't. Granted, I'm sitting here in the midst of this event and still trying to get "traction" on all that you're spewing. God Blake, you have me reeling and worried about your mental state.

At some point you have to get back to your life.

Again, I'm beside myself with worry as to your state of mind and angry. Angry that you don't see

how obsessed you are becoming, how scary you're
sounding and how detrimental this line of thinking is.

Stop, Blake. Just STOP!

Tara

"I must possess all, or I possess nothing"

— Skeletor

Dear Tara,

I have painfully noticed your missing xo at the end of letters for some time. I know I have made you angry, resulting in the loss of our little written affections. I am sorry.

Trying to convey my anger without engaging yours has proven difficult, considering the two contrasting worlds we occupy. You are in a place where constant compassion is necessary to deal with the pain around you. I am removed from the darkness in that perspective. But try to understand there is something in that very darkness reaching me way up here. I talked to George and he told me IRS agents stopped by his place to see if he knew anything about my whereabouts. He and Justin know I am on vacation, but thankfully they don't know where. George's leg is still on the mend and he feigned being a bit loopy from the medication, so their visit was short lived. He thought he was helping me out with the snoopy government dudes and I didn't tell him otherwise. When he asked me where I was, I just made it sound like it was on a "need-to-know basis" and we both got a good laugh from that one. But, the thing is Tara, these guys are still looking for me, months after the fact. And it makes me wonder how they would even know about George. Justin I can understand, but George was a new electrician who had just started at the Towers about a week before I was laid off. He went out for drinks once with me and a few of the other guys. And sure, I contacted him to see how he was after I got word from Juan he had been hurt. But it's not like we were good buddies or anything. Granted, I called to see how he was doing, but the only reason I knew his number was because it's the same as my home number with the last two digits transposed. Somehow every stone is being turned. It makes me worry that someday they might show up at your door, though that hardly seems possible. How fortunate you weren't listed in my address book. Then again, George wasn't either. I would do anything to make sure they never find out about your existence, or any connection to me. I can't imagine any way that is possible. But they aren't giving up on finding me, and it makes me really believe it would be to silence me. Like my worst fear, what probably happened to Joe that night.

I'm glad I had enough foresight not to dip into my bank account. I think that could have led them in this direction in no time. Which reminds me...and you know I hate to ask Tara, but do you think you could send a little more money? I'm running low and I hate to ask Rob for any more. He really has been so good and supportive in every way. You know I will pay you back with interest, and that my real wish is that all the money we have will someday be "our money." But I need to stay alive for that, my dear.

It occurred to me that my rent hasn't been paid in two months. I'm reluctant to call Mrs. Ward but given I need to before she sells all my stuff, I guess I have to call her sooner than later.

For now, I'm so appreciative of your being there and supporting me when I know sometimes I make that real hard. This indebtedness makes our recent communications even sadder.

Look, I'm not sitting up here just creating crazy conspiratorial scenarios, though I know it sometimes sounds like that to you. I'm here watching the news, and very curious about all I see. Granted with Rob's help and amazing intelligence, we uncover things that just don't make sense. Yes, I'm more curious than most, WITH MY LIFE ON THE LINE. If what I suspect is correct, that our government had something to do with 9/11, who can I trust? Who do I turn to? Could I go to the media when they appear to be complicit in this whole thing? In fact I don't think such deluding of glaring facts would be possible without their compliance. Look at the recent news that Fox Management gives their affiliates "talking" points. The information Fox Management wants to be sure is out there is distributed via memo every morning. And if one of their stations doesn't comply? Pink slips are handed out. How about the reporter who had a favorable interview with Hillary Clinton? When it was strongly suggested to the General Manager of the station not to run the piece, and the station ran the interview anyway? Both the General Manager and reporter were summarily fired. Fair and Balanced? Bullshit.

You want me to go to the authorities? Which authorities? What would I tell them? I saw explosives in the Towers before 9/11, oh yeah, and I was shot at. But when I tried to get the police to go to the Towers, I was too chicken to join them, because I think my best friend was shot and feared for my own life. And there were strange men at my apartment door when I tried to go home. Oh, and then I didn't call back because I figured I could handle this when I got back from Maine. Who is going to believe I saw explosives before 9/11? Even if they still have my initial report on file, my only proof is Joe, and he is dead. I'd either end up in a rubber room or at the bottom of the East River.

And Building 7? The way you asked the question, "Building what?" That is how it feels when no one is talking about it, or even seems to know it came down that very day. Don't you understand how they HAD TO bring that building down? How it was probably the main staging area for a demolitions operation that morning. And after the shock lingering trauma of that fateful morning, it quietly comes down at free fall speed that evening and hardly anyone knows. It was just close enough to orchestrate the destruction, yet far enough away to be safe. And then poof! Gone is any evidence. If it weren't so utterly horrible, I'd say it was a brilliant plot. Goddamn them!! For the sake of argument let's say this wasn't the base of operations. Don't you find it highly unlikely that several other buildings, much closer in proximity to the Towers, all with more fires, much more damage, didn't collapse? By the Fire Chief's own words, "Building 7 had a few fires." Watch the various clips from that fateful day and you'll see reporters standing right out in front of Building 7 delivering the news. I'm to believe a building declared a "safe zone" for reporters to broadcast from, comes tumbling down? Scratch that — DEMOLITIONED!

Fire brought it down? A few small fires? All the firemen were in other buildings where fires were blazing. I'm sorry you can't see it Tara. I don't want to call and start arguing with you about all this over a public phone.

Did you hear what Bush had to say today? "I think we can all say the past is over." Huh? What a brilliant orator. I'm sorry, I've gotten to the point where I despise him. Not that I think he had the brains to think anything like this up. It's just that he seems to be the perfect puppet. It makes me wonder more about that shady election we just went through not too many months ago. Now he's telling all America 'bout them evildoers in that phony Southern drawl of his. Did you know he is from Massachusetts? I heard him speaking very eloquently in debates and speaking engagements before he was installed into the Presidency. I wonder if this nightmare would have even happened if the man who really got the most votes became our President.

I believe Cheney, Rumsfeld, and a few other choice individuals either planned this attack or knew of the terrorists' plans. They were complicit (Cheney's stand down orders). They had talked about what it would take to bring the U.S. into a war. That they needed something as catastrophic as Pearl Harbor to occur in order to get us into Afghanistan, and even Iraq. Not only did that occurring "Pearl Harbor" event happen less than eight months into the Presidency ("Wag The Dog," anyone?), but it gave them the opportunity to enact a freedom-consuming bill like the Patriot Act, put boots on the ground in Afghanistan, develop another "Big Brother" organization, Homeland Security, and put fear in the hearts and minds of every citizen.

How about that ridiculous color-coded alert system? Watch how that will be used right up to the next election. Probably Red Alerts right before we vote.

But the War Machine is already rolling and it seems nobody, but its drivers, have anything to say about it.

This is precisely what they wanted, and it's beyond disgusting. With the admission of the missing 2 trillion dollars wiped from the front pages the morning after. Where did that money go to? Was it used for this "Pearl Harbor"-like operation?

Yeah, the so-called Liberal Media is sure plugging a lot of holes for this Right Wing War Machine. Common sense doesn't seem to be in play here. Like FOX NEWS, they are being told to stick to a script that doesn't allow hard questions to be asked. Scared and frightened, the American people are being sold a bill of goods. I would probably be sitting right where most Americans are if I hadn't seen those explosives, or been thrown into this situation where I can sit and critically look at all we're being shown. It's pretty apparent there's a big hand choking the collective throats of Americans. Insisting on war, and denying us our liberties. Tara, this whole event was like a well-wrapped gift for this administration. Only they bought, wrapped and presented the gift, I'm sure. You just have to understand how they are the only ones who benefit from this tragedy.

I wish I didn't know, but now that I do, I can't not know.

I am so in love with you Tara. Please see how this is a situation wrought with fear and anxiety for me. The biggest lie ever concocted, and perpetrated on our fellow Americans by our own government.

And I, Blake Watson, a speck in the scheme of things, am privy to all their wickedness wrought. They don't want me alive. I'm sure of that. Their Achilles heal is Building 7. Maybe Building 7's demise will find its way to light. Will the "smoking gun" unravel this well-hidden "false flag" operation? Will others soon see that this stuff doesn't add up?

I can't carry this load without you. I know I might sound crazy to you…but PLEASE!! Don't give up on us now.

OX,

Blake

P.S. Don't give up on us Tara.

"The more a human creature has tasted
of bitter things the more it hungers
after the sweet things of life"

— Maxim Gorky

Blake,

I love you too.

There's no getting around that fact. I do love you.

Hard to say that knowing how short a period of time we've known each other. Yet I knew the moment I looked into your eyes at that Starbucks.

There was a spark.

A passion.

A knowing...

But, the lack of phone calls, the constant back and forth as to what happened on 9/11 has put a strain on our relationship. Maybe because you haven't witnessed the devastation first hand, maybe because you weren't here to help put up flyers or offer solace when we were looking for Carol... maybe because there's a measure of wanting you here right beside me that hasn't been addressed or fulfilled. Maybe it's because instead of working on getting out of Maine, you're instead doing research on something you have no control over. Maybe it's because you don't realize that you can't hide up there in Maine for the rest of your life. Maybe it's that I picture you and Rob sitting up there in easy chairs with beers in hand, bantering conspiracy theories back and forth. Maybe it's because Christmas is in two days and you've been gone since August. AUGUST, Blake! Maybe it's because of all of these things that I just don't have the strength any more to continue. While you have brought up a couple of solid points that can't be easily explained away, I just think not everything can fit so neatly into your predetermined scenario. Ultimately I don't believe our government was party to any of what happened on 9/11 (I find the theory of our government's involvement ridiculous). What further complicates matters is not knowing when you'll be returning to the city or IF you will return.

You're probably not coming back and after many restless nights of worrying this over and over in my head, I can't continue to hold onto a relationship that no longer exists.

I know with only Rob and me in your life this is going to come as a surprise and most likely unwelcome news. Even as I write this I'm crying. There's a little voice in the back of my head that says "don't let him go." It's the one that holds you close to my heart. There's another louder voice that is saying "this is doomed." It could be years down the road before we even have a chance at a relationship and right now there's just so much drama and hurt and pain....

I've enclosed $250. Maybe Rob can make a trip down here to dip into your checking/savings account. I know you don't want to show any transactions coming from Maine, so I have to assume this is the only way to get your money. I'm sorry this will be the last you'll hear from me, and the last money order I send, but hope you understand how I have to move on. Please don't feel as if you need to repay me.

You're a great guy Blake and I'm sorry to leave you like this, but it seems I can't help you. Nor can I wait around hoping you'll help yourself.

Be safe.

Be well.

All my love,

Tara

"The cave you fear to enter holds
the treasure you seek"

— Joseph Campbell

———◆———

Tara Please…

This can't be happening. That you would say these words, "I can't continue to hold onto a relationship that no longer exists." I just can't accept that was you. Tell me this isn't happening. My heart is sinking faster than the rocks I throw into the lake.

Please Tara, I'm begging you. I can't handle this. Our love is life changing. I won't let a situation that is World changing, that we had nothing to do with, take away the most wonderful person I have ever known. You must listen to that voice in the back of your head…the one that is telling you "don't let him go." That is your heart talking, my love. Don't you dare listen to the other voices I hear coming through you. Those are the voices of disappointment and anger. We will never be "doomed" and I am not ever going to let that happen. I don't care if my life is in danger. I will come to the city before I let you go. The fear of what you are saying has our far-too-short life together passing before my eyes.

Sweet baby, do you remember our second date? When we were supposed to meet your friends but just wanted to spend the evening alone together, and detoured through Central Park? We came upon that Mexican restaurant that was closing. When you asked if they were closed she said, "Yes", but asked us to wait a minute. Then she went to the kitchen and came back telling us we could have our choice of three things we could order to go, even though they were closed. When I found out the two of you had only met once before, I was surprised and remembered feeling like I was with someone who was liked by so many. Nothing like that would ever happen for me. When I would go out someplace I'd never know any of the staff even if they had been there for years and wore a nametag. It was just a little something that said a whole lot about you.

You bring joy to people's lives. Not just with the most beautiful smile ever, that you wear like an angel for most everybody, but you show an interest in everybody's life you come into contact with. I know what people think when they see you. It's the sweetest relief a kind heart can bring.

I can't let you go, Tara. I won't! Don't take the most special person I have ever known from me. You are my hope, my world, and the one I was sure I could count on in this most horrible of events.

I should have called you more often. I'm so sorry. In fact, I've tried to reach you several times after reading your letter.

My obsession about the things I uncovered with Rob blinded me to your needs. It is okay if you don't believe me about those things. I have to respect what you feel and I have strayed from that. I can see where my priorities became distorted and betrayed my heart blindly, while hurting the one I care about most. I need you so.

I'm not going to go to the authorities, but try to carve out a new life under an assumed name. Rob has a friend who has a friend…He's going to ask for a new Social Security number and license for himself. Even though his picture will be on it he has a way in which to exchange it with my photo. We just need to make sure there is no trace back to me. We are also looking into the possibility of getting a license and work papers from Canada. It would probably be safer being from another country. Whatever the case, the bottom line is I'm trying to get my life back Tara. A life that includes you. Please don't let us go.

OX OX OX OX OX OX OX OX

Blake

"To hurt is as human as to breathe"

— J. K. Rowling

———◆———

Tara,

It's New Year's Day and I can't believe I haven't been able to reach you. Please Tara. You don't know how I'm feeling. This hurt is beyond what I can bear. Not you…the one I was so sure of…the one I was too sure of. I'm so sorry and I'm begging you to reconsider. I've tried calling you several times and I'm not sure if you're avoiding me or I'm just not catching you at home. I know you can't call me, but I've tried your number in the morning and at night. Each ring that goes unanswered is a driving pain of emptiness I can't bear.

You didn't respond to my recent letter…That sends chills and heartaches through me that feel like knives. Please tell me it's not too late, my love.

OX,

Blake

"It is a miserable state of mind to have few things to desire and many things to fear"

— Francis Bacon

Tara,

Tara, please, please, please. You must stop this separation. My heart is breaking here. I still can't reach you. No word from you. What can I say? What can I say to make you see I'm sorry? So, very, very, sorry.

Do you remember our "special" getaway weekend?? Our last night there when neither one of us could fall asleep? We just gave up on that and went to the living room and talked for hours. We stretched out together on the couch and told each other everything. The way we felt about each other and how we couldn't believe it could be this wonderful.

Of course our relationship has been mired by my predicament and I should have been focusing more on how to go forward through such difficulties. Even the fact that men are looking for me shouldn't present a situation that our love can't endure.

That weekend, that night when we were curled up on the couch you looked me in the eyes and said there was no one who made you feel more safe, more loved, more recognized for who you are. I treasure that memory. It was the most loving and secure moment I have ever felt in my life.

Has this tragedy been so bad and my behavior so unforgiving that you would change those feelings? I refuse to believe it.

I know my letters about 9/11 have troubled you, and probably made you wonder if I was the same guy you fell in love with. I am the same man, Tara. Who would have known things could go this awry? Even though I do believe our government had something to do with this, and even though I have seen evidence to show things don't add up, as they would have us believe, I am sitting here feeling removed from all I have felt so strongly about. It all seems to mean nothing without you. Like I said to you once, "I can't not know what I know," but now I wish I didn't know. I wish I hadn't seen those explosives. But that wish doesn't change the fact that my life is still in danger. It's just that my life doesn't hold the meaning it did without you…

Without you? I have to block that thought, and that thought has become my life. It fights me when I need to eat…when I need to sleep…when I need to be at peace remembering the love we have shared.

Please Tara, answer my letters. Please answer my calls. I'm trying to get my new identity. I've already taken steps to change my appearance. I've done all of this in the hopes we can still find our way…still share that life we dreamed. It is not possible to be in this world without you. I can't let go. I can't erase the picture of your smile that hangs so heavy in my heart. Please Tara, forgive me and come back to me.

I'm here, right here, waiting for your response.

OX,

Blake

P.S. I'm rereading all your letters over and over again. Trying to decipher at what point did I go wrong. Tara, please…

"There's a wall between you and what
you want and you got to leap it"

— Bob Dylan

—◆—

Tara,

I'm about out of my mind. I tried to call you last night at 1 A.M. and still no answer. I'm hoping this daily barrage of letters and constant calls will convince you of my commitment. My NEED to make this right.

My heart is burning at the thought there could be someone new in your life. If that is the case then all my worst fears will have come to render this life meaningless. But I only want what's best for you, and if it is someone who you love and cherish the way you did me, then I will have to step aside. Maybe you have found a better man for you. These thoughts find me at the end of my rope, and I will let go of that rope if it is tied to someone new. Tell me this isn't the case Tara. Tell me what my heart is literally dying to hear. I'm so sorry for not telling you enough how much I love you. If my fears are wrong and there is hope, I will, and can do, whatever you wish to bring us back together. The fear of losing you is far greater than the fear of those men finding me.

Don't leave me this way...

OX,

Blake

"The big lesson in life, baby, is never
be scared of anyone or anything"

— Frank Sinatra

Blake,

I wanted to contact you so I called Rob's house. I didn't leave a message because I'm unsure if he's going to the cabin often so here I am writing this letter. See how hard this is? The fact that I can't get a hold of you has been, at times, extremely difficult. It's one of the reasons I stepped away.

I've missed you. I've missed you terribly, Blake. I was hoping time apart would render you but a nice thought in my memory. The truth of the matter is I find myself yearning for you more.

I didn't take your calls because I was trying to get "over" you. I didn't write back because I was trying to distance myself from you. I figured it would only be a matter of time when I'd forget about you and the special bond we had. It would only be a matter of time before my heart stopped aching for you. But, this hasn't proved to be true.

Several things have happened which prompted this letter. IRS agents came to my workplace asking if I knew where you were. I told them I didn't know a "Blake Watson." Fortunately Mona was working and asked "who?" The IRS agents said they had it on good authority that I was dating a "Blake Watson" and they were looking for him. Mona snorted and said, "Honey, if this little gal was dating anyone, I would be the first to know." I laughed. I hoped that the gerbil running loops in my stomach wasn't visible from the outside. I was absolutely frightened.

How did they find out about me? Who told them? The only one I can think of that even knew of me in your life is Mrs. Ward. They could have returned to find out if she heard anything from you. Given her response the first time they showed up, why would she tell them anything? Why would she mention me to them? I wanted to go over and ask her, but dare not do anything. Instead, I came home, took a long hot bath, considered everything you've written, said and now after having seen these guys face-to-face? I'm certain you are right. These guys are not IRS agents. Maybe I'm being too hypersensitive, but there was just something off-putting about them. I didn't ask for credentials, not wanting to tip my hand. Why would I care where they were from if I don't know the person they are trying to reach. Right?

The scary thing is I can't come up with one good reason why they would be looking for you if not for those explosives you saw. They mean to keep you quiet, just as you suspected.

There's something else I need to tell you. Another reason for my turnaround on all you and Rob uncovered. I watched a special on all the people who perished on 9/11. They were giving about 3 seconds to every person and underneath their photograph was listed their name and whether the individual was "Missing" or "Dead."

As they alphabetically went through the names, I saw many familiar names on the list. It was particularly hard to see Carol Willard's name and picture. All in all, it was devastating to watch, and a painful reminder of that day. When they came to "G," Joe Grabowski's photograph was there large as life with his name listed right above "Dead." Not having met Joe I stared at the name, looked at his picture and only had a second to register "it's Joe."

My mouth fell open.

I mean, all this time I've been telling you that Joe was probably hiding out like you were, but they listed him as dead? Uncertain that I really saw Joe's name, I called a couple of places starting with the TV station. I learned the list was compiled by Homeland Security. I then called Homeland Security and asked how a name got on the list. They explained how the morgue provides them with positive identification on the bodies. Homeland Security verifies the information. They don't run their own DNA test, but they have experts who review the same material as the morgue in making their determination. Once received and confirmed, the name is put on the list.

I then confirmed that indeed it was Joe Grabowski I saw on the special. My God, somehow someone was able to get his name on the list. Blake, do you know what this means? Well, of course you know what this means. You've suspected it all along and while I saw truth in some of what you were saying, this is just another finger solidly pointing at our government. Local or national, there is no way your friend Joe went from weeks of missing to conveniently showing up for work on the morning of 9/11. There is no question in my mind now. Federal, state, local, some government agency had a hand in putting Joe's name on the list.

I guess your fears were warranted. Joe did die that night in the Towers and to make sure there was no question as to his demise, they listed him as dead due to the 9/11 attacks. What his mother must be going through. Imagine, being told your son died that day when he'd been missing weeks before. I guess they don't care what one hysterical mother is going to say. Why bother caring about Mrs. Grabowski when it's evident they didn't care about one single person who died that day. All for the cause, right? Who's going to listen to Mrs. Grabowski now?

I'm fearful now more than ever, but more important, I'm pissed. Pissed that all you and Rob have uncovered just might be the truth to what happened to our city. I'm pissed that our government might have had a hand in this and livid that so many died that day, including one of my best friends.

Fuck them! I know you have never heard me swear because I don't usually go down this path but FUCK! My fear quickly turned to anger and I'm ready to expose these guys. Let's do it Blake. Let's expose these murderous assholes. Let's gather all the information you and Rob have and put it out there.

What I've doubted all these months is the level this went to. I doubted our government's involvement and thought you could blindly go to Homeland Security with your information. I'm so glad you were smart enough not to listen to me. Had you gone to Homeland Security, I'm pretty sure the special I saw the other night would have had you listed as dead. Oh Blake, I'm so sorry. It's one thing to think a fringe fraction is after you, it's another to realize it's one's own government! The resources, the reach, the efforts they will go to!

Did you hear? Cheney and Rumsfeld want to enact war on Iraq. A Pentagon official told them "no." He said they couldn't use the 9/11 attacks as reason to go to war with Iraq because there is no link to Iraq, at all. In the article I read, several came out and said the Pentagon official (wish I could remember his name) was very brave. Many are questioning Cheney and Rumsfeld's motives, but as soon as I read that news item I thought of how you questioned whether we would eventually go to war with Iraq. I pooh-poohed this idea knowing that most of the terrorists came from Saudi Arabia. Why go to Iraq, I reasoned? How are they going to sell THAT initiative? I guess they weren't able to sell it to the Pentagon. At least, yet. I don't doubt they will eventually get us into war with Iraq. No more doubts in this mind!

Reason doesn't seem to be part of the mainstay these days and while there are many who say we shouldn't go into Iraq, the very question raises more questions. Your research on Cheney and his "Pearl Harbor type war" rings true. I'm frightened, Blake.

I'm going to end this here so I can get this letter in the mail. <u>Call me soon!</u> Any time. I promise, this time I'll pick up.

Let's expose these bastards, Blake. Let's turn this country on its side and speak the truth about who was involved in 9/11.

I love you Blake and am more scared for you now than ever.

XO

Tara

"I will drink the wine while it is warm
And never let you catch me
looking at the sun
And after all the loves of my life
After all the loves of my life,
you'll still be the one"

— Jimmy Webb

———•———

My Dear Tara,

I am over the moon to hear from you my love. The sweetest relief I have ever known. I didn't want to go on if you weren't going to be by my side. I have been in survival mode, grateful to make it here to now.

God, I love you so.

Now I see you in my mind. Your smile just across the room, welcoming me to taste your kisses again. To be wrapped in the comfort of your angel arms once more. When I leave this Earth I pray they will be holding me.

Yet still, I want to thwart the forces that coldly want to squash this dream for their ill-gotten murderous gains.

You and I found each other for a larger reason than has yet been revealed.

Rob went fishing without me. My company has been more depressing than the bass hanging helpless on the end of his line. He came down to the cabin to deliver your letter, not knowing if it contained good news or bad. Last week he told me I was going to have to get used to not having you in my life. That I had to concentrate on what I was doing and how I was going to keep myself safe in my "I don't care anymore" state. He is down at the dock getting ready to go out but I'm sure he, and the fish at the bottom of the lake, heard my joyful yell.

There may be hundreds of miles between us but you are "right here" beside me again, Tara.

I will have my papers in two weeks. Who knew it would take this long? Still, we may be standing together sooner than you think. I will call you tonight.

I want to call you right now, but I know you are still at work. I don't know why I am even writing this as I am going to start walking to the phone booth as soon as I am done. I guess if I need a reason, it is so you will always have this loving reminder of how you made me feel this day.

On the other hand…there's a fist to my throat! Joe listed as dead? My dear friend, Joe? He was one of my best friends. To be honest, it's not really a shock. Ever since I learned his mother filed that missing person's report, ever since someone picked up his phone yet no one answered? The handwriting was on the wall. You, sweet angel, gave me a glimmer of hope that he may be hiding out like me, but I guess I kind of knew the worst was true. It's obvious they just decided to suck him into the mass killing perpetrated that day. Ah Tara, while I reconciled that Joe was probably dead, having it confirmed like this is another shock to my system. I'm sure his mother is at the police station right now trying to get someone to listen to her that her son couldn't possibly have been among the dead since he was missing well before 9/11. They'll probably pat her hand and send her on her way thinking she's delusional. Who's going to bother to check? Who has the time to delve into Joe's disappearance and then subsequent "death notification" when the city is still dealing with the aftermath of this horrible tragedy? I was thinking of calling her, but how can I? Since I didn't share how we were shot at at the Towers that night, how can I possibly call her now?

I wish I had never run into Joe that night. Wow, that was the last time I would ever see him. God, Tara.

There are many troubling waters to swim…

Mrs. Ward hasn't heard from me in so long, much less received a rent check in three months that she has probably gotten rid of my stuff and rented the apartment. After your leaving letter I was so over-wrought, I never did get around to calling her.

As you know, I have been frightened to get money out of my bank account for fear they could trace me here. I'm considering taking one big withdrawal one second before I get on the road to start my new life.

I hope you will be a part of my new life, Tara. I know it's asking a lot, but having you by my side would make this life worth living. I'll talk more to you about this when I call which is all of 30 minutes away! That is, if you head straight home from work.

Recently I have seen protesters on the news with signs reading "No Blood For Oil." That must be what this is all about. Iraq has the second largest oilfield in the world, next to Bush's good buddies, and our old friends and allies, the Saudis.

Here I go again, piling on the stuff you don't want to hear..The stuff that drove you away from me just a short while ago. I'm going to start walking down to the library to use their phone. It's still early, but I want to hear your voice as soon as possible.

Long before you read this, our voices will be dancing together on the telephone...

Thank you for coming back to me, Tara

I LOVE YOU SO,

OX OX OX OX

Blake

"I believe in your eyes
I believe in your fate
I believe we can fly
On the wings that we create"

— Melissa Etheridge

Blake,

I'm glad we talked. It was so good to hear your voice and did you notice how we couldn't stop talking over each other? I know I scared you by going away Blake, I'm so sorry.

I've given some thought about going away with you. It's easy to just say "yes" because we do have this special, deep connection. I hope you understand though, why I needed to take a little time to think about it. We've really only known each other a couple of months! Why, before you left for Maine we'd only been dating for five weeks, and yes, we saw each other every night and talked constantly, and yes, I feel as if I know you completely. As you said in one of your previous letters, it was almost as if fate had us in hand right from the start. I remember the coffee shop and your kindness in helping me pick up my change, but most of all I remember the spark of recognition when we started to talk to one another. Remember? Our connection was immediate.

I was blessed the day you came into my life Blake. It's just that going away with you is a big step. The future unknown. Where will we live? How will we survive? What if "IRS agents" show up? How often do we move? Is your new identity good enough?

There are a million and one questions and yes, it's scary to think of this big unknown future when for so long I've had my future planned out.

I went to art school, started as an intern at the gallery and have finally made a dent in the art world. My opinion is valued, and I'm called in for consultations with some of the top art critics. I'm living my dream in what once was my dream city.

Going away with you also means that I cut off communication with all my family, all my friends. I can't say I won't ever see them again, but it's pretty close to "never," since we don't know where we'll end up and we don't know when, if ever, we'll return.

We both agree the government will never stop looking for you, Blake. We have to go with that truth and (literally) run with it.

So after much consideration I've decided to join you. How can I not? I love you Blake and the thought of not having you in my life is unfathomable. You are my best friend and the one I want to spend time with.

I love who you are and who I am in your presence.

I always thought I would choose independence over dependence, a career over a man, yet here I am forging a different path. I don't see me as being dependent upon you as much as you and I are shouldering what this world has to throw at us. I don't see myself as choosing you over a career path. I see it more as I'm going to live my life by following my heart.

It's going to be hard. I've decided to share the truth with my mother. To disappear without her knowing why I left will kill her. I must tell her the truth. She will DEFINITELY keep our secret, and will find a version of the truth that will help my dad understand. As for my sisters, brother, cousins, aunts, uncles, etc., my mom and I will figure out a plausible reason for my departure. Don't know what this will be, but my mom is really good at thinking outside the box and will figure something out.

As for my friends, I'm going to tell them that I've been offered a job in Rome at the Vatican to archive and update their artwork. It's a dream job and one they know I would jump at. In fact, the Vatican went through a private recruiter last year to find such a person. Unfortunately they didn't come to me, but I plan on telling my friends that after an exhaustive search with no results, they came crawling to little ole' Tara. Given the sensitivity of my new employer and being in another country, etc. it will be easy to fade away.

I can't wait to see you at our "special" place. You'll probably get there before me. Work wasn't happy I only gave two weeks notice and convinced me to stay three. So, I've got another two weeks left. It pains me not to be there when I said, but I really hate to leave them in the lurch. I have no choice at this time.

I want to do so much in the city before leaving. I want to go to Elaine's because I've never been there. I want to take a ferry out to the Statue of Liberty because, believe it or not, I've never done that, either. I want to do a million things before leaving here because I doubt we'll ever be back in the NY area.

Can't believe we're making this move. Can't believe **I'm** making this move with someone I haven't known that long. But how long does one need to know someone to know they are in love?

We should address the issue of Rutherford. Dear Rutherford. He's pretty skittish as it is and I can't imagine him enjoying car rides and new places to live. If indeed, we're forced to go on the run. Maybe he'll get use to that kind of life, but I'm wondering instead if I should find a home for him here. Perhaps Mrs. Ward will take him. He's your cat, Blake, so whatever you want to do is fine. Remember though that I'm coming to you by bus.

I do like Rutherford. He's now sleeping on my legs. I've been waking up to the slight weight of him on my legs and his soft, contented purr. He still won't let me touch him, but he no longer gives me a surly look when he realizes I'm awake. That's right! No longer does he quickly jump off the bed and give me a snide look! I figure it'll take another four months before he allows me to pet him. Eight months before he allows me to pick him up!

I found out something that will be of interest to you. Come to find out the part of the Pentagon that was hit by the "plane?" It housed the Resources Services of Washington department. In this department worked civilian accountants, bookkeepers and budget analysts. By all accounts, the paper trail for the missing two trillion dollars was contained in this department. So let's see, on 9/10 Rumsfeld announces over two trillion dollars is missing from the Pentagon. On the very next day a catastrophic event occurs. By mere coincidence all the accounting records that would have been sorted through to figure out where the two trillion dollars went just happens to be in the Resources Services of Washington Department which just happened to be on the flight path of the plane that went into the Pentagon? Thirty-four of sixty-five of the casualties that day at the Pentagon were working in this department and where do you think the paperwork is? Gone. Can't be traced. Good-bye $2 trillion; this is just the price we paid for those nasty terrorists and their planes.

Wow, look at me, joining the conspiracy theorists! I think I'd like to rework that terminology. Look at me exposing PROPOGANDA.

I went down to Ground Zero this morning and your point about Building 7 was driven home. You're right. There were other buildings that sustained much more damage than Building 7. At least, when I look at the images of Building 7 an hour before it collapsed and then look at the other surrounding buildings — it's unfathomable how this building went down. It was securely far enough away from the Towers! Another thing that I found interesting is Building 3. You were right (again), a huge chunk of steel fell on Building 3's roof, causing the top five floors to look as if they were split in half. The metal chunk was being removed this morning and loaded up on a truck.

I asked a couple of firefighters how it is that Building 3 sustained a huge fire, when Building 7, with just a few fires, went down? It didn't make sense to me. The firefighters looked at each other with "knowing" glances and told me there was no official explanation for why Building 7 came down. When I asked them if it was possible jet fuel melted the steel in the Towers they shook their heads "no" and changed the subject. One firefighter said it wasn't "safe" to talk about any of this and the others agreed. It's understandably a touchy subject for them.

Oh God, Blake, all of this hurts. It's obvious those firefighters knew something was amiss. It's obvious others are questioning the official account and yet here I sit with more information than most, no longer questioning. Saddened though. Saddened by all that has been wrought and all that dare not be said for fear of losing one's life.

I can't wait to learn what your new name is going to be. I love the name Blake Watson! In fact, it sounds a bit like a soap opera stars name. Dr. Blake Watson to emergency — STAT! I can't imagine having to assume a new identity. That's going to be hard, yet I guess when you consider the alternative, one doesn't mind going by a new name. I think you're right to hold out for the Canadian papers. Even though it's a bit more $ and takes a little longer to get, I think it's safer.

Which by the way, the enclosed money order should help.

Glad I don't have to come up with a new identity!

I know we're going to be talking so this letter will probably not be necessary, and in fact given I'll be seeing you in two and a half weeks (2-1/2 weeks!) this may be my last letter to you.

Have you kept all my letters? I've kept all yours and plan to bring them along with me. Yes, I know we have to travel light, but to me, having your letters/our letters will stand as a testament to what transpired all these months when our world literally came crumbling down. I'm not proud of some of the questions I had for you in earlier letters, and yes, I still question some of the things you and Rob uncovered, but…

Well, for sentimental reasons I'm going to bring your letters with me. Okay, got to run. Suzanne and Michele are arriving soon. We're going to dinner and a movie.

Love you, Blake

XO

Tara

P.S. I wrote down what you told me Congressman Jim McDermott said, "You can make people do anything if they're afraid." I'd like to take that statement further by asserting you can also make people believe anything when they are afraid!

"You want to save humanity,
But it's people that you just can't stand"

— John Lennon

My Tara,

How wonderful to hear your voice again last night. Even when you fell asleep…how tired you must be from all you have had to deal with, and all you have had to consider. I could hear your soft breathing over the phone, and I imagined you were lying next to me again. "Someday Soon" as the song goes…I didn't want to wake you but knew I must, to say "goodnight."

I hadn't thought about how difficult a decision I was asking you to make, to go away with me. Just worrying that you ever would. I want to drop to my knees and thank you for the trust in our love, and for the courage you, my love, possess. I was worried about having your mom know what we are doing, but so impressed with your ingenious idea on what to tell the rest of your family and friends. I think it will be good to have a secret ally at your home, and no one better to trust with the secret our path is going to take. I am so lucky to have you in my life. I can't imagine dealing with what is to come if you weren't.

A part of me wishes I could hold Mrs. Grabowski in her pain, and tell her why her son was such a great friend, and remind her again what she knows so well, but you're right. Talking to her now serves no means. It's best to have her think, however she finds it hard to believe, that Joe perished that day in the Towers. Joe was a great man who loved her so much. He never moved away from her life, like I have wondered why I did from my own family, so many times. If I live to see the Truth we know unveiled, I will remember him in some "formal" way to the awakened world. I love you, Joe, whatever better place you are in.

Rob is in Ohio visiting his family. Before he left, we agreed I would call him. Why? He plans on visiting my mom to tell her everything that is going on and I want to be sure the conversation went well. I just got off the phone with him, and by his account everything went well. He took her out to lunch and unloaded the whole story. She was overwhelmed. Then, as the contradictions of what the TV has told her so convincingly were weighed, she became angry that no one else is questioning these things. I wonder if any of this information will ever find its way to the only outlet that matters, our TVs. "How is it possible?" Mom asked.

Rob explained that this was an attack on our Homeland, and Americans have never had to deal with that before. The closest thing we ever had was Pearl Harbor, and this was worse than that in lives lost. He said that even with all we uncovered, many would find it hard to accept our government had anything to do with 9/11. It's just the way we are wired, he reasoned.

We need people like Rob who question; who take a critical eye to what we're told and see things aren't adding up.

My poor mother, what a burden for her to bear. Like your own mother, there is no one we can better trust to keep our secret. But at this point in their lives would they have ever thought this could be possible?

It occurred to me after getting off the phone with Rob if perhaps "they" are watching my mom's house. After the "IRS" agents made their appearance several times there looking for me, why not? It would be the most logical place to keep an eye out for me. I didn't want to worry Rob by calling him back to ask and besides, I know he is smart enough to be thinking that on his own.

You know, he wasn't even going to visit his family till next month but knowing the paperwork for my new identity is coming soon, he moved his trip up. He left this morning to make the drive back here, but plans on stopping a couple of places along the way, so he'll be back in a couple of days. I'm looking forward to hearing more about his visit to my hometown.

Did I tell you, Rob has plans to post the things we've uncovered on the internet. He wants to show pictures of the hole in the Pentagon not being as wide as the wingspan of the plane that supposedly struck it, the terrorists passport, footage of the Towers coming down in their own footprint (especially Building 7!), next to footage of demolition and collapsed building. He even wants to include footage of Rumsfeld's speech the night before about the $2 trillion. He'll have links to news articles, documents, etc. etc. He believes that all people need to see is the massive evidence collected on one website and they'll start to come around. Well, some of them will. I worry about his website being traced back to him. Can you post these things, without it being traced?

Did you know the steel from the Twin Towers is being shipped overseas and melted down? Isn't that some kind of material evidence to the biggest crime scene ever? Who is paying attention to any of this??

You've heard this all before, Tara. I'm just here with a lot of time on my hands, writing a letter to you.

I do have some other news that is timing-wise, not good. And there is nothing that can be done about it. The cabin has been rented this weekend. I'm not happy about it so close to our departure. I can't complain as I've benefited so much from my little hideout here in the woods. But these places exist to be rented and a couple of hunters have taken this one for the weekend. I'm going to head down to Rob's house. I don't know why I feel exposed there, but I do. I mean its Maine. There aren't that many residents around here, and Rob has a pretty good piece of land around his property. I just like the anonymity of this cabin tucked away in the woods.

There is some goods news too. Rob fixed up an old Impala Station Wagon and gave it to me. He says if we keep the oil changed, it will run forever. The man who owned it had put only 15,000 thousand miles on it. He kept it undercover in his barn and it is in pristine condition. He went into a nursing home and Rob picked it up for a song. Rob doesn't want any money for it either.

How am I ever gonna repay this guy? I have been thinking about this lately. Will I ever see him again? I would someday love for you to meet him too. Maybe he will come and visit us one day. It's odd to think he is the only person on the planet who will know my identity and where we're going.

Okay Tara, I'm going to end this here. I've got to get my stuff out of here and make it look like someone hasn't been staying in the cabin. Not that the hunters would care, but I just feel better leaving things as I found them when Rob first brought me here. Huh, how do I make it look DUSTY! HA!

Look forward to talking to you again soon, Tara.

OX,

Blake

"There are only two mistakes one can make along the road to truth. Not going all the way and not starting"

— Buddha

Dear Tara,

I'm sorry I didn't call. You won't believe what has happened. Just when I thought all I had to look forward to is for us to be together again, and my exit at last from Maine, the bottom falls out of my world again.

Rob got back from Ohio yesterday. An hour after he returned, guess who showed up at his house to pay a visit. The IRS guys! Yes, the IRS guys!!! I was afraid they were watching my mom's house for my possible return, and that must be just what happened. When Rob went to see my mom to take her out for lunch, they must have gotten his license plate, and all the information they needed to lead them here. Hell, he may have even been followed for eight hundred miles. It doesn't matter; all that matters is they were here in Maine. I'm just damn glad I wasn't at his house when they came. I had a feeling staying there while he was away was a bad idea, and I guess my intuition is survival fed.

Rob told them he hadn't seen me in years, doing his best to act surprised at their appearance, and cool like nothing was wrong. He joked to them "what, has Blake skipped out on paying his taxes?" And they said, "Something like that," and gave him a card with a number to call if he sees me. My blood ran cold when Rob told me this. I don't really know if they believed him or even if they are still around. He said he thought they bought it, but what if that was their ploy? What if they find out he is the caretaker for the cabins? What if they actually show up here?

I'm so paranoid Tara, I can't stand it. I'm also worried to death for Rob. He has pretty much saved my life, and I could be putting his own in danger.

He is going to check on my new identification tomorrow, thinking it might be ready. A part of me is so sad to say goodbye to him, and another part is screaming, "Get out of here, now."

I don't want to talk about this anymore so I'm gonna change the subject to the other nightmare I lived through over the weekend. I spent the entire weekend in my new "home on the road"…the Impala.

As I mentioned, I didn't want to stay at Rob's (good thing!), so I spent my days hanging out at the library, and deep in the woods during the night. I was so bitter cold at times because I didn't want to run the engine very long just in case there might be an exhaust leak in the Impala. I would have loved to have gotten out to build a fire but I was afraid maybe some Ranger might see it and wonder what I was doing way out there. It is mighty cold up here at night in Maine. It must have been in single digits.

I would have given anything to have your warm body next to mine.

I'm back at the cabin now, but my little sanctuary in the woods has more of a pins and needles feel about it that is so foreign to me here. I'm not going down to the library or the payphone anymore. To be honest I haven't left the cabin at all.

I just want my new identity! Once I have it in hand, I'm on the road.

Wish I didn't know what I know.

I'm reminded of the old saying, "Ignorance Is Bliss."

I hope we can come back here someday, Tara. You've heard me talk about it but you really have to see it and experience it. I told him I would miss him so much and that I was really sorry for all the time, all the years, I had let go by without visiting. How strange it is that it took such a tragedy to bring us together again. I told him that my leaving didn't mean we wouldn't see each other again soon. We talked about trying to start a kind of "group thing" for people who have uncovered the truth about 9/11. Of course there must be more of us out there in the country... and cyberland. How is it possible we're the only ones who have found this out?

To be continued...

Hello again My Dear...

It is morning. I had to stop writing this letter last night because Rob came by. My heart sank, thinking the "IRS" agents had returned, but instead he pointed to the full moon and asked if I wanted to go fishing one last time. In the cloak of darkness, having an opportunity to get out of the cabin where I've been holed up for days, I took him up on his offer. As I was laying down the letter he walked over and said, "Here this came for you," and laid my new identity in my hand. Then said, "I think you'll be needing this too, so we can keep in touch," and laid a new cell phone in my other hand. I started to cry, and gave him a big hug. I love this guy!

Rob said, "Make sure you give me a call if those IRS agents catch up with you," and we both laughed, me through my tears.

As we were fishing, we reminisced about the insanity of the last seven months. How we uncovered so much information, unveiling a story so different than the one our country, and much of the "free world," has been forced to swallow.

Rewarding in enlightenment, yet painful to acknowledge.

I am leaving in a little while, Tara. But there are a few things I want to say to you before I go. I have written much to you from this cabin and this will be the last letter I write from here.

I need to thank you again for changing your life for a guy like me. For believing in me. For finding your way back to me, through all your anger and pain that my letters drove you to these last months. It is not lost on me the blessing you are in my life. I hope I can be the same for you. I will find happiness for you, or die trying. Don't take that the wrong way. A life in hiding won't be easy.

I sometimes wonder if I should have stayed in NY and taken care of business, never leaving your side. But isn't it strange how fearing for your life will make you do things you never thought possible? Soon we will meet up in our very special place. I would like to think we will make our home there, but that remains to be seen.

Wow, 2002 with you…no one else will do.

I promise to write you better lines that rhyme than that little ditty. But right now it says it all. Meet me in our embrace, my love. I will call you tonight from the road…

OX,

Blake

"I love her and that's the beginning
and ending of everything"

— F. Scott Fitzgerald

My love,

Our first piece of mail in our new place!

Are you surprised to see a letter from me? I trust the mailman will deliver this even though you may not have arrived at the house yet.

Odd to think this is the last piece of written communication for us.

If my calculations are correct, we are three short days and two long nights from being together.

This letter is not to continue our discussion about our government, what happened on 9/11, your new identity, or any of the wrangling we've danced with these past months. We know what we need to do. If not for the thousands that died on 9/11, if not for having learned the truth…I don't think I would have the fortitude to do what we've planned. This isn't the life Tara Young from little ole' NJ had in mind when she set out to conquer the art world. Who knew I'd be working alongside the man I love to ensure the truth is known by every citizen of this country. How can I not? How can I not when so

Publisher's Note: This letter was found unopened in the stack we were provided. We assume Tara arrived before the letter. At least, this is one explanation for it not having been read.

many lives were taken? When families were ripped apart? And for what? Greed. Domination. It doesn't matter whatever their motivating factor was, for in the end many lost their lives.

Ah, here I am stating that I need not go into this, and nonetheless getting into it! Errrrr! It just sets my blood boiling! I am glad we've worked out a way to get the message out and teach others what we know. I know our efforts will all be behind the scenes, and liken it in some regards to the Underground Railroad. Yet, as you keep pointing out and are acutely aware — our first consideration must be for our safety.

Our safety is of the utmost importance to me. Particularly now that we're being entrusted with another life on this planet that we need to ensure is safe and secure.

Yes Blake, I'm pregnant.

I was going to tell you months ago, but obviously the timing wasn't right.

I'm seven months pregnant.

The past two nights when we've talked for hours, I've wanted to blurt out the news, but then our conversation would take a turn and the next thing you know, I'm rethinking when to tell you.

Yes, Blake, we're pregnant.

You're going to be a father.

While you may not be ready to be a husband, I hope you're ready to be a father. It's the reason I'm writing this to you now. You say you love me. You say you want me with you always. For me, knowing I'm carrying your child changed things. It changed the way I view you, made me rethink everything about you. Perhaps this is the reason why I was struggling so hard with the 9/11 information you and Rob kept uncovering. With Carol gone, Joe missing, your friends and family being visited by IRS agents and the devastation and despair all around me...then to learn I'm pregnant with your child? I wanted you back in my arms, out of harm's way and I wanted you to hold me, love me, tell me everything was okay. That you welcome this child into your heart.

That you welcome me into your heart.

I'm afraid you may think this child a burden. You may rethink how you feel about me. I want to give you these three short days and two long nights to consider how you feel about it all.

We've only known each other a short while and these past few months have been extremely difficult. I figure if we weathered this, we weathered it all.

Yet you need to decide.

If you aren't at the house when I arrive on the 17th, I'll stay until the morning of the 19th. If you aren't there by the 19th, I'll return to the city to raise our baby. S/he will have all the advantages of living in the big city. They will be much loved by my family and friends. Of course, s/he will be spoiled rotten by me! I won't tell him/her of you until asked. I'll explain that you are on a secret mission, a journey and only share the full truth once s/he is older.

If you are at the house when I arrive, please know that you still reserve the right to not welcome this baby or me in your life. I know some men who hightail it down the road as soon as they learn a baby is coming. I don't think you are this type of man, Blake. Yet don't know if your feelings for me change with a baby on the way.

I'm taking a leap of faith here, Blake.

I hope you'll see my baby bump and tenderly embrace me, and this new life we created. I understand how learning about our child is not only a shock for you, but to consider raising a baby while possibly being on the run for quite some time…well, I can understand if you, and ultimately "we," decide its best you travel alone.

I hope you open up your arms, your heart, and your very soul to be my partner for life. From every pore of my soul, I know you are the man I love. The man I want to spend my time with. The person I want to wake up to, to see what the day holds. Through your eyes, your imagination, your spirit, your heart. If I could be so blessed to spend my time in the company of YOU...

I love you, Blake.

Tara

By the Lake
Illustration of Blake Watson by Rob Boswell

Here is a subset of the list Rob Boswell provided:

AE911truth.org

911truth.org

911sharethetruth.org

Communitycurrency.org

consensus911.org

CSI911.info

Firefightersfor911truth.org

flybynews@hughes.net

GlobalOutlook.ca

Imagineourworldunited.net

jerrypippin.com/CON-files911

Meria.net

OC911truth.com

pilotsfor911truth.org

pl911truth.com

postmark911.com

StL911.truth.info

wanttoknowinfo.com

Whyitishard.com

MOVIES

9/11: Explosive Evidence — Experts Speak Out, by AE911Truth

9/11: Blueprint for Truth — The Architecture of Destruction, by AE911Truth

9/11 In Plane Site

9/11 Mysteries

9/11 Press for Truth

9/11 Remembered

The Conspiracy to Rule the World: from 911 to the Illuminati

Denial Stops Here: From 9-11 to Peak Oil and Beyond

Fool Me Once: A New World Order Agenda for 2012

Inside Job: Unmasking the 9/11 Conspiracies

Loose Change 9/11: An American Coup

The New Pearl Harbor

The Truth and Lies of 9-11

Zero: An Investigation Into 9/11

"What Is To Give Light
Must Endure Burning"

— Viktor Frankl

Made in the USA
Monee, IL
07 July 2026